Space Tug

Murray Leinster

Contents

SPACE TUG

BY

Murray Leinster

To Joan Patricia Jenkins

30 MINUTES TO LIVE!

Joe Kenmore heard the airlock close with a sickening wheeze and then a clank. In desperation he turned toward Haney. "My God, we've been locked out!"

Through the transparent domes of their space helmets, Joe could see a look of horror and disbelief pass across Haney's face. But it was true! Joe and his crew were locked out of the Space Platform.

Four thousand miles below circled the Earth. Under Joe's feet rested the solid steel hull of his home in outer space. But without tools there was no hope of getting back inside. Joe looked at his oxygen meter. It registered thirty minutes to live.

Space Tug by Murray Leinster is an independent sequel to the author's popular *Space Platform*, which is also available in a POCKET BOOK edition. Both books were published originally by Shasta Publishers.

Of other books by Murray Leinster, the following are science-fiction:

1

To the world at large, of course, it was just another day. A different sort entirely at different places on the great, round, rolling Earth, but nothing out of the ordinary. It was Tuesday on one side of the Date Line and Monday on the other. It was so-and-so's wedding anniversary and so-and-so's birthday and another so-and-so would get out of jail today. It was warm, it was cool, it was fair, it was cloudy. One looked forward to the future with confidence, with hope, with uneasiness or with terror according to one's temperament and one's geographical location and past history. To most of the human race this was nothing whatever but just another day.

But to Joe Kenmore it was a most particular day indeed. Here, it was the gray hour just before sunrise and already there were hints of reddish colorings in the sky. It was chilly, and somehow the world seemed still and breathless. To Joe, the feeling of tensity marked this morning off from all the other mornings of his experience.

He got up and began to dress, in Major Holt's quarters back of that giant steel half-globe called the Shed, near the town of Bootstrap. He felt queer because he felt so much as usual. By all the rules, he should have experienced a splendid, noble resolution and a fiery exaltation, and perhaps even an admirable sensation of humility and unworthiness to accomplish what was expected of him today. And, deep enough inside, he felt suitable emotion. But it happened that he couldn't take time to feel things adequately today.

He was much more aware that he wanted some coffee rather badly, and that he hoped everything would go all right. He looked out of the windows at empty, dreary desert under the dawn sky. Today was the day he'd be leaving on a rather important journey. He hoped that Haney and the Chief and Mike weren't nervous. He also hoped that nobody had gotten at the fuel for the pushpots, and that the slide-rule crew that had calculated everything hadn't made any mistakes. He was also bothered about the steering-rocket fuel, and he was uncomfortable about the business of releasing the spaceship from the launching cage. There was, too, cause for worry in the take-off rockets--if the tube linings had shrunk there would be some rather gruesome consequences--and there could always be last-minute orders from Washington to delay or even cancel everything.

In short, his mind was full of strictly practical details. He didn't have time to feel noble aspirations or sensations of high destiny. He had a very tricky and exacting job ahead of him.

The sky was growing lighter outside. Stars faded in a paling blue and the desert showed faint colorings. He tied his necktie. A deep-toned keening set up off to the southward, over the sere and dreary landscape. It was a faraway noise, something like the lament of a mountain-sized calf bleating for its mother. Joe took a deep breath. He looked, but saw nothing. The noise, though, told him that there'd been no cancellation of orders so far. He mentally uncrossed one pair of fingers. He couldn't possibly cross fingers against all foreseeable disasters. There weren't enough fingers--or toes either. But it was good that so far the schedule held.

He went downstairs. Major Holt was pacing up and down the living room of his quarters. Electric lights burned, but already the windows were brightening. Joe straightened up and tried to look casual. Strictly speaking, Major Holt was a family friend who happened also to be security officer here, in charge of protecting what went on in the giant construction Shed. He'd had a sufficiently difficult time of it in the past, and the difficulties might keep on in the future. He was also the ranking officer here and consequently the immediate boss of Joe's enterprise. Today's affair was still highly precarious. The whole thing was controversial and uncertain and might spoil the career of somebody with stars on his collar if it should fail. So nobody in the high brass wanted the responsibility. If everything went well, somebody suitable would take the credit and the bows. Meanwhile Major Holt was boss by default.

He looked sharply at Joe. "Morning."

"Good morning, sir," said Joe. Major Holt's daughter Sally had a sort of understanding with Joe, but the major hadn't the knack of cordiality, and nobody felt too much at ease with him. Besides, Joe was wearing a uniform for the first time this morning. There were only eight such uniforms in the world, so far. It was black whipcord, with an Eisenhower jacket, narrow silver braid on the collar and cuffs, and a silver rocket for a badge where a plane pilot wears his wings. It was strictly practical. Against accidental catchings in machinery, the trousers were narrow and tucked into ten-inch soft leather boots, and the wide leather belt had flat loops for the attachment of special equipment. Its width was a brace against the strains of acceleration. Sally had had much to do with its design.

But it hadn't yet been decided by the Pentagon whether the Space Exploration Project would be taken over by the Army or the Navy or the Air Corps, so Joe wore no insignia of rank. Technically he was still a civilian.

The deep-toned noise to the south had become a howl, sweeping closer and trailed by other howlings.

"The pushpots are on the way over, as you can hear," said the major detachedly, in the curious light of daybreak and electric bulbs together. "Your crew is up and about. So far there seems to be no hitch. You're feeling all right for the attempt today?"

"If you want the truth, sir, I'd feel better with about ten years' practical experience behind me. But my gang and myself--we've had all the training we can get without an actual take-off. We're the best-trained crew to try it. I think we'll manage."

"I see," said the major. "You'll do your best."

"We may have to do better than that," admitted Joe wrily.

"True enough. You may." The major paused. "You're well aware that there are--ah--people who do not altogether like the idea of the United States possessing an artificial satellite of Earth."

"I ought to know it," admitted Joe.

The Earth's second, man-constructed moon--out in space for just six weeks now--didn't seem nowadays like the bitterly contested achievement it actually was. From Earth it was merely a tiny speck of light in the sky, identifiable for what it was only because it moved so swiftly and serenely from the sunset toward the east, or from night's darkness into the dawn-light. But it had been fought bitterly before it was launched. It was first proposed to the United Nations, but even discussion in the Council was vetoed. So the United States had built it alone. Yet the nations which objected to it as an international project liked it even less as a national one, and they'd done what they could to wreck it.

The building of the great steel hull now out there in emptiness had been fought more bitterly, by more ruthless and more highly trained saboteurs, than any other enterprise in history. There'd been two attempts to blast it with atomic bombs. But it was high aloft, rolling grandly around the Earth, so close to its primary that its period was little more than four hours; and it rose in the west and set in the east six times a day.

Today Joe would try to get a supply ship up to it, a very small rocket-driven cargo ship named Pelican One. The crew of the Platform needed food and air and water--and especially the means of self-defense. Today's take-off would be the first attempt at a rocket-lift to space.

"The enemies of the Platform haven't given up," said the major formidably. "And they used spectroscopes on the Platform's rocket fumes. Apparently they've been able to duplicate our fuel."

Joe nodded.

Major Holt went on: "For more than a month Military Intelligence has been aware that rockets were under construction behind the Iron Curtain. They will be guided missiles, and they will carry atom bomb heads. One or more may be finished any day. When they're finished, you can bet that they'll be used against the Platform. And you will carry up the first arms for the Platform. Your ship carries half a dozen long-range interceptor rockets to handle any attack from Earth. It's vitally important for them to be delivered."

"They'll attack the Platform?" demanded Joe angrily. "That's war!"

"Not if they deny guilt," said the major ironically, "and if we have nothing to gain by war. The Platform is intended to defend the peace of the world. If it is destroyed, we won't defend the peace of the world by going to war over it. But while the Platform can defend itself, it is not likely that anyone will dare to make war. So you have a very worthwhile mission. I suggest that you have breakfast and report to the Shed. I'm on my way there now."

Joe said, "Yes, sir."

The major started for the door. Then he stopped. He hesitated, and said abruptly, "If my security measures have failed, Joe, you'll be killed. If there has been sabotage or carelessness, it will be my fault."

"I'm sure, sir, that everything anybody could do--"

"Everything anybody can do to destroy you has been done," said the major grimly. "Not only sabotage, Joe, but blunders and mistakes and stupidities. That always happens. But--I've done my best. I suspect I'm asking your forgiveness if my best hasn't been good enough."

Then, before Joe could reply, the major went hurriedly away.

Joe frowned for a moment. It occurred to him that it must be pretty tough to be responsible for the things that other men's lives depend on--when you can't share their danger. But just then the smell of coffee reached his nostrils. He trailed the scent. There was a coffeepot steaming on the table in the dining-room. There was a note on a plate.

Good luck. I'll see you in the Shed.

Sally

Joe was relieved. Sally Holt had been somewhere around underfoot all his life. She was a swell girl, but he was grateful that he didn't have to talk to her just now.

He poured coffee and looked at his watch. He went to the window. The far-away howling was much nearer, and dawn had definitely arrived. Small cloudlets in a pale blue sky were tinted pinkish by the rising sun. Patches of yucca and mesquite and sage out beyond the officers' quarters area stretched away to a far-off horizon. They were now visibly different in color from the red-yellow earth between them, and cast long, streaky shadows. The cause of the howling was still invisible.

But Joe cared nothing for that. He stared skyward, searching. And he saw what he looked for.

There was a small bright sliver of sunlight high aloft. It moved slowly toward the east. It showed the unmistakable glint of sunshine upon polished steel. It was the artificial satellite--a huge steel hull--which had been built in the gigantic Shed from whose shadow Joe looked upward. It was the size of an ocean liner, and six weeks since some hundreds of pushpots, all straining at once, had gotten it out of the Shed and panted toward the sky with it. They'd gotten it twelve miles high and speeding eastward at the ultimate speed they could manage. They'd fired jato rock-ets, all at once, and so pushed its speed up to the preposterous. Then they'd dropped away and the giant steel thing had fired its own rockets--which made mile-long flames--and swept on out to emptiness. Before its rockets were consumed it was in an orbit 4,000 miles above the Earth's surface, and it hurtled through space at some-thing over 12,000 miles an hour. It circled the Earth in exactly four hours, fourteen minutes, and twenty-two seconds. And it would continue its circling forever, need-ing no fuel and never descending. It was a second moon for the planet Earth.

But it could be destroyed.

Joe watched hungrily as it went on to meet the sun. Smoothly, unhurriedly, serenely, the remote and twinkling speck floated on out of sight. And then Joe went back to the table and ate his breakfast quickly. He wolfed it. He had an appointment to meet that minute speck some 4,000 miles out in space. His appointment was for a very few hours hence.

He'd been training for just this morning's effort since before the Platform's launching. There was a great box swinging in twenty-foot gimbal rings over in the Shed. There were motors and projectors and over two thousand vacuum tubes, re-lays and electronic units. It was a space flight simulator--a descendant of the Link trainer which once taught plane pilots how to fly. But this offered the problems and the sensations of rocketship control, and for many hours every day Joe and the three members of his crew had labored in it. The simulator duplicated every sight and sound and feeling--all but heavy acceleration--to be experienced in the take-off of a rocketship to space. The similitude of flight was utterly convincing. Sometimes it was appallingly so when emergencies and catastrophes and calamities were staged in horrifying detail for them to learn to respond to. In six weeks they'd learned how to handle a spaceship so far as anybody could learn on solid ground--if the simulator was correctly built. Nobody could be sure about that. But it was the best training that could be devised.

In minutes Joe had finished the coffee and was out of Major Holt's quarters and headed for the Shed's nearest entrance. The Shed was a gigantic metal structure ris-ing out of sheer flat desert. There were hills to the westward, but only arid plain to the east and south and north. There was but one town in hundreds of miles and that was Bootstrap, built to house the workmen who'd built the Platform and the still invisible, ferociously howling pushpots and now the small supply ships, the first of which was to make its first trip today.

The Shed seemed very near because of its monstrous size. When he was actually at the base of its wall, it seemed to fill half the firmament and more than half the horizon. He went in, and felt self-conscious when the guard's eyes fell on his uniform. There was a tiny vestibule. Then he was in the Shed itself, and it was enormous.

There were acres of wood-block flooring. There was a vast, steel-girdered arching roof which was fifty stories high in the center. All this size had been needed when the Space Platform was being built. Men on the far side were merely specks, and the rows of windows to admit light usually did no more than make a gray twilight inside. But there was light enough today. To the east the Shed's wall was split from top to bottom. A colossal triangular gore had been loosened and thrust out and rolled aside, and a doorway a hundred and fifty feet wide let in the sunshine. Through it, Joe could see the fiery red ball which was the sun just leaving the horizon.

But there was something more urgent for him to look at. Pelican One had been moved into its launching cage. Only Joe, perhaps, would really have recognized it. Actually it was a streamlined hull of steel, eighty feet long by twenty in diameter. There were stubby metal fins--useless in space, and even on take-off, but essential for the planned method of landing on its return. There were thick quartz ports in the bow-section. But its form was completely concealed now by the attached, exterior take-off rockets. It had been shifted into the huge cradle of steel beams from which it was to be launched. Men swarmed about it and over it, in and out of the launching cage, checking and rechecking every possible thing that could make for the success of its flight to space.

The other three crew-members were ready--Haney and Chief Bender and Mike Scandia. They were especially entitled to be the crew of this first supply ship. When the Platform was being built, its pilot-gyros had been built by a precision tool firm owned by Joe's father. He'd gone by plane with the infinitely precise apparatus to Bootstrap, to deliver and install it in the Platform. And the plane was sabotaged, and the gyros were ruined. They'd consumed four months in the building, and four months more for balancing with absolute no-tolerance accuracy. The Platform couldn't wait so long for duplicates. So Joe had improvised a method of repair. And with Haney to devise special machine-tool setups and the Chief to use fanatically fine workmanship, and Mike and Joe aiding according to their gifts, they'd rebuilt the apparatus in an impossibly short time. The original notion was Joe's, but he couldn't have done the job without the others.

And there had been other, incidental triumphs by the team of four. They were not the only ones who worked feverishly for the glory of having helped to build the Earth's first artificial moon, but they had accomplished more than most. Joe had even been appointed to be an alternate member of the Platform's crew. But the man he was to have substituted for recovered from an illness, and Joe was left behind at the Platform's launching. But all of them had rated some reward, and it was to serve in the small ships that would supply the man-made satellite.

Now they were ready to begin. The Chief grinned exuberantly as Joe ducked through the bars of the launching cage and approached the ship. He was a Mohawk Indian--one of that tribe which for two generations had supplied steel workers to every bridge and dam and skyscraper job on the continent. He was brown and bulky and explosive. Haney looked tense and strained. He was tall and lean and spare, and a good man in any sort of trouble. Mike blazed excitement. Mike was forty-one inches high and he was full-grown. He had worked on the Platform, bucking rivets and making welds and inspections in places too small for a normal-sized man to reach. He frantically resented any concessions to his size and he was as good a man as any. He simply was the small, economy size.

"Hiya, Joe," boomed the Chief. "All set? Had breakfast?"

Joe nodded. He began to ask anxious questions. About steering-rocket fuel and the launching cage release and the take-off rockets and the reduction valve from the air tanks--he'd thought of that on the way over--and the short wave and loran and radar. Haney nodded to some questions. Mike said briskly, "I checked" to others.

The Chief grunted amiably, "Look, Joe! We checked everything last night. We checked it again this morning. I even caught Mike polishing the ejection seats, because there wasn't anything else to make sure of!"

Joe managed a smile. The ejection seats were assuredly the most unlikely of all devices to be useful today. They were supposedly life-saving devices. If the ship came a cropper on take-off, the four of them were supposed to use ejection-seats like those supplied to jet pilots. They would be thrown clear of the ship and ribbon-parachutes might open and might let them land alive. But it wasn't likely. Joe had objected to their presence. If a feather dropped to Earth from a height of 600 miles, it would be falling so fast when it hit the atmosphere that it would heat up and burn to ashes from pure air-friction. It wasn't likely that they could get out of the ship if anything went wrong.

Somebody marched stiffly toward the four of them. Joe's expression grew rueful. The Space Project was neither Army nor Navy nor Air Corps, but something that so far was its own individual self. But the man marching toward Joe was Lieutenant Commander Brown, strictly Navy, assigned to the Shed as an observer. And there were some times when he baffled Joe. Like now.

He halted, and looked as if he expected Joe to salute. Joe didn't.

Lieutenant Commander Brown said, formally: "I would like to offer my best wishes for your trip, Mr. Kenmore."

"Thanks," said Joe.

Brown smiled distantly. "You understand, of course, that I consider navigation essentially a naval function, and it does seem to me that any ship, including a space-ship, should be manned by naval personnel. But I assuredly wish you good fortune."

"Thanks," said Joe again.

Brown shook hands, then stalked off.

Haney rumbled in his throat. "How come, Joe, he doesn't wish all of us good luck?"

"He does," said Joe. "But his mind's in uniform too. He's been trained that way. I'd like to make a bet that we have him as a passenger out to the Platform some day."

"Heaven forbid!" growled Haney.

There was an outrageous tumult outside the wide-open gap in the Shed's wall. Something went shrieking by the doorway. It looked like the magnified top half of a loaf of baker's bread, painted gray and equipped with an air-scoop in front and a plastic bubble for a pilot. It howled like a lost baby dragon, its flat underside tilted up and up until it was almost vertical. It had no wings, but a blue-white flame spurted out of its rear, wobbling from side to side for reasons best known to itself. It was a pushpot, which could not possibly be called a jet plane because it could not possibly fly. Only it did. It settled down on its flame-spouting tail, and the sparse vegetation burst into smoky flame and shriveled, and the thing--still shrieking like a fog-horn in a tunnel--flopped flat forward with a resounding *clank!* It was abruptly silent.

But the total noise was not lessened. Another pushpot came soaring wildly into view, making hysterical outcries. It touched and banged violently to earth. Others appeared in the air beyond the construction Shed. One flopped so hard on landing that its tail rose in the air and it attempted a somersault. It made ten times more noise than before--the flame from its tail making wild gyrations--and flopped back again with a crash. Two others rolled over on their sides after touching ground. One ended up on its back like a tumble-bug, wriggling.

They seemed to land by hundreds, but their number was actually in dozens. It was not until the last one was down that Joe could make himself heard. The pushpots were jet motors in frames and metal skin, with built-in jato rocket tubes besides their engines. On the ground they were quite helpless. In the air they were unbelievably clumsy. They were actually balanced and steered by vanes in the blasts of their jets, and they combined the absolute maximum of sheer thrust with the irreducible minimum of flyability.

Crane-trucks went out to pick them up. Joe said anxiously, "We'd better check our flight plan again. We have to know it absolutely!"

He headed across the floor to the flight data board. He passed the hull of another ship like his own, which was near completion, and the bare skeletons of two others which needed a lot of work yet. They'd been begun at distant plants and then hauled here on monstrous trailers for completion. The wooden mockup of the design for all the ships--in which every possible arrangement of instruments and machinery had been tested out--lay neglected by the Shed wall.

The four stood before the flight data board. It listed the readings every instrument should show during every instant of the flight. The readings had been calculated with infinite care, and Joe and the others needed to know them rather better than they knew their multiplication tables. Once they started out, they wouldn't have time to wonder if everything was right for the time and place. They needed to know.

They stood there, soaking up the information the board contained, forming mental pictures of it, making as sure as possible that any one of them would spot anything wrong the instant it showed up, and would instantly know what had to be done about it.

A gigantic crane-truck came in through the wide doorway. It dangled a pushpot. It rolled over to the launching cage in which the spaceship lay and set the unwieldy metal object against that cage. There was a *clank* as the pushpot caught hold of the magnetic grapples. The crane went out again, passing a second crane carrying a second pushpot. The second beetle-like thing was presented to the cage. It stuck fast. The crane went out for more.

Major Holt came across the floor of the Shed. It took him a long time to walk the distance from the Security offices to the launching cage. When he got there, he looked impatiently around. His daughter Sally came out of nowhere and blew her nose as if she'd been crying, and pointed to the data board. The major shrugged his shoulders and looked uneasily at her. She regarded him with some defiance. The major spoke to her sternly. They waited.

The cranes brought in more pushpots and set them up against the steel launching cage. The ship had been nearly hidden before by the rocket tubes fastened outside its hull. It went completely out of sight behind the metal monsters banked about it.

The major looked at his watch and the group about the data board. They moved away from it and back toward the ship. Joe saw the major and swerved over to him.

"I have brought you," said the major in an official voice, "the invoice of your cargo. You will deliver the invoice with the cargo and bring back proper receipts."

"I hope," said Joe.

"*We* hope!" said Sally in a strained tone. "Good luck, Joe!"

"Thanks."

"There is not much to say to you," said the major without visible emotion. "Of course the next crew will start its training immediately, but it may be a month before another ship can take off. It is extremely desirable that you reach the Platform today."

"Yes, sir," said Joe wrily. "I have even a personal motive to get there. If I don't, I break my neck."

The major ignored the comment. He shook hands formally and marched away. Sally smiled up at Joe, but her eyes were suddenly full of tears.

"I--do hope everything goes all right, Joe," she said unsteadily. "I--I'll be praying for you."

"I can use some of that, too," admitted Joe.

She looked at her hand. Joe's ring was on her finger--wrapped with string on the inside of the band to make it fit. Then she looked up again and was crying unashamedly.

"I--will," she repeated. Then she said fiercely, "I don't care if somebody's looking, Joe. It's time for you to go in the ship."

He kissed her, and turned and went quickly to the peculiar mass of clustered pushpots, touching and almost overlapping each other.

He ducked under and looked back. Sally waved. He waved back. Then he climbed up the ladder into Pelican One's cabin. Somebody pulled the ladder away and scuttled out of the cage.

The others were in their places. Joe slowly closed the door from the cabin to the outer world. There was suddenly a cushioned silence about him. Out the quartz-glass ports he could see ahead, out the end of the cage through the monstrous doorway to the desert beyond. Overhead he could see the dark, girder-lined roof of the Shed. On either side, though, he could see only the scratched, dented, flat undersides of the pushpots ready to lift the ship upward.

"You can start on the pushpot motors, Haney," he said curtly.

Joe moved to his own, the pilot's seat. Haney pushed a button. Through the fabric of the ship came the muted uproar of a pushpot engine starting. Haney pushed another button. Another. Another. More jet engines bellowed. The tumult in the Shed would be past endurance, now.

Joe strapped himself into his seat. He made sure that the Chief at the steering-rocket manual controls was fastened properly, and Mike at the radio panel was firmly belted past the chance of injury.

Haney said with enormous calm, "All pushpot motors running, Joe."

"Steering rockets ready," the Chief reported.

"Radio operating," came from Mike. "Communications room all set."

Joe reached to the maneuver controls. He should have been sweating. His hands, perhaps, should have quivered with tension. But he was too much worried about too many things. Nobody can strike an attitude or go into a blue funk while they are worrying about things to be done. Joe heard the small gyro motors as their speed went up. A hum and a whine and then a shrill whistle which went up in pitch until it wasn't anything at all. He frowned anxiously and said to Haney, "I'm taking over the pushpots."

Haney nodded. Joe took the over-all control. The roar of engines outside grew loud on the right-hand side, and died down. It grew thunderous to the left, and dwindled. The ones ahead pushed. Then the ones behind. Joe nodded and wet his lips. He said: "Here we go."

There was no more ceremony than that. The noise of the jet motors outside rose to a thunderous volume which came even through the little ship's insulated hull. Then it grew louder, and louder still, and Joe stirred the controls by ever so tiny a movement.

Suddenly the ship did not feel solid. It stirred a little. Joe held his breath and cracked the over-all control of the pushpots' speed a tiny trace further. The ship wobbled a little. Out the quartz-glass windows, the great door seemed to descend. In reality the clustered pushpots and the launching cage rose some thirty feet from the Shed floor and hovered there uncertainly. Joe shifted the lever that governed the vanes in the jet motor blasts. Ship and cage and pushpots, all together, wavered toward the doorway. They passed out of it, rocking a little and pitching a little and wallowing a little. As a flying device, the combination was a howling tumult and a horror. It was an aviation designer's nightmare. It was a bad dream by any standard.

But it wasn't meant as a way to fly from one place to another on Earth. It was the first booster stage of a three-stage rocket aimed at outer space. It looked rather like--well--if a swarm of bumblebees clung fiercely to a wire-gauze cage in which lay a silver minnow wrapped in match-sticks; and if the bees buzzed furiously and lifted it in a straining, clumsy, and altogether unreasonable manner; and if the appearance and the noise together were multiplied a good many thousands of times-- why--it would present a great similarity to the take-off of the spaceship under Joe's command. Nothing like it could be graceful or neatly controllable or even very speedy in the thick atmosphere near the ground. But higher, it would be another matter.

It *was* another matter. Once clear of the Shed, and with flat, sere desert ahead to the very horizon, Joe threw on full power to the pushpot motors. The clumsy-seeming aggregation of grotesque objects began to climb. Ungainly it was, and clumsy it was, but it went upward at a rate a jet-fighter might have trouble matching. It wobbled, and it swung around and around, and it tipped crazily, the whole aggregation of jet motors and cage and burden of spaceship as a unit. But it rose!

The ground dropped so swiftly that even the Shed seemed to shrivel like a pricked balloon. The horizon retreated as if a carpet were hastily unrolled by magic. The barometric pressure needles turned.

"Communications says our rate-of-climb is 4,000 feet a minute and going up fast," Mike announced. "It's five.... We're at 17,000 feet ... 18,000. We should get some eastward velocity at 32,000 feet. Our height is now 21,000 feet...."

There was no change in the feel of things inside the ship, of course. Sealed against the vacuum of space, barometric pressure outside made no difference. Height had no effect on the air inside the ship.

At 25,000 feet the Chief said suddenly: "We're pointed due east, Joe. Freeze it?"

"Right," said Joe. "Freeze it."

The Chief threw a lever. The gyros were running at full operating speed. By engaging them, the Chief had all their stored-up kinetic energy available to resist any change of direction the pushpots might produce by minor variations in their thrusts. Haney brooded over the reports from the individual engines outside. He made minute adjustments to keep them balanced. Mike uttered curt comments into the communicator from time to time.

At 33,000 feet there was a momentary sensation as if the ship were tilted sharply. It wasn't. The instruments denied any change from level rise. The upward-soaring complex of flying things had simply risen into a jet-stream, one of those wildly rushing wind-floods of the upper atmosphere.

"Eastern velocity four hundred," said Mike from the communicator. "Now four-twenty-five.... Four-forty."

There was a 300-mile-an-hour wind behind them. A tail-wind, west to east. The pushpots struggled now to get the maximum possible forward thrust before they rose out of that east-bound hurricane. They added a fierce push to eastward to their upward thrust. Mike's cracked voice reported 500 miles an hour. Presently it was 600.

At 40,000 feet they were moving eastward at 680 miles an hour. A jet-motor cannot be rated except indirectly, but there was over 200,000 horsepower at work to raise the spacecraft and build up the highest possible forward speed. It couldn't be kept up, of course. The pushpots couldn't carry enough fuel.

But they reached 55,000 feet, which is where space begins for humankind. A man exposed to emptiness at that height will die just as quickly as anywhere between the stars. But it wasn't quite empty space for the pushpots. There was still a very, very little air. The pushpots could still thrust upward. Feebly, now, but they still thrust.

Mike said: "Communications says get set to fire jatos, Joe."

"Right!" he replied. "Set yourselves."

Mike flung a switch, and a voice began to chatter behind Joe's head. It was the voice from the communications-room atop the Shed, now far below and far behind. Mike settled himself in the tiny acceleration-chair built for him. The Chief squirmed to comfort in his seat. Haney took his hands from the equalizing adjustments he had to make so that Joe's use of the controls would be exact, regardless of moment-to-moment differences in the thrust of the various jets.

"We've got a yaw right," said the Chief sharply. "Hold it, Joe!"

Joe waited for small quivering needles to return to their proper registrations.

"Back and steady," said the Chief a moment later. "Okay!"

The tinny voice behind Joe now spoke precisely. Mike had listened to it while the work of take-off could be divided, so that Joe would not be distracted. Now Joe had to control everything at once.

The roar of the pushpots outside the ship had long since lost the volume and timbre of normal atmosphere. Not much sound could be transmitted by the near-vacuum outside. But the jet motors did roar, and the sound which was not sound at such a height was transmitted by the metal cage as so much pure vibration. The walls and hull of the spaceship picked up a crawling, quivering pulsation and turned it into sound. Standing waves set up and dissolved and moved erratically in the air of the cabin. Joe's eardrums were strangely affected. Now one ear seemed muted by a temporary difference of air pressure where a standing wave lingered for a second or two. Then the other eardrum itched. There were creeping sensations as of things touching one and quickly moving away.

Joe swung a microphone into place before his mouth.

"All set," he said evenly. "Brief me."

The tinny voice said:

"You are at 65,000 feet. Your curve of rate-of-climb is flattening out. You are now rising at near-maximum speed, and not much more forward velocity can be anticipated. You have an air-speed relative to surface of six-nine-two miles per hour. The rotational speed of Earth at this latitude is seven-seven-eight. You have, then, a total orbital speed of one-four-seven-oh miles per hour, or nearly twelve per cent of your needed final velocity. Since you will take off laterally and practically without air resistance, a margin of safety remains. You are authorized to blast."

Joe said:

"Ten seconds. Nine ... eight ... seven ... six ... five ... four ... three ... two ... one...."

He stabbed the master jato switch. And a monstrous jato rocket, built into each and every one of the pushpots outside, flared chemical fumes in a simultaneous, gigantic thrust. A small wire-wound jato for jet-assisted-take-off will weigh a hundred and forty pounds and deliver a thousand pounds of thrust for fourteen seconds. And that is for rockets using nonpoisonous compounds. The jatos of the pushpots used the beryllium-fluorine fuel that had lifted the Platform and that filled the take-off rockets of Joe's ship. These jatos gave the pushpots themselves an acceleration of ten gravities, but it had to be shared with the cage and the ship. Still....

Joe felt himself slammed back into his seat with irresistible, overwhelming force. The vibration from the jets had been bad. Now he didn't notice it. He didn't notice much of anything but the horrible sensations of six-gravity acceleration.

It was not exactly pain. It was a feeling as if a completely intolerable and unbearable pressure pushed at him. Not only on the outside, like a blow, but inside too, like nothing else imaginable. Not only his chest pressed upon his lungs, but his lungs strained toward his backbone. Not only the flesh of his thighs tugged to flatten itself against his acceleration-chair, but the blood in his legs tried to flow into and burst the blood-vessels in the back of his legs.

The six-gravity acceleration seemed to endure for centuries. Actually, it lasted for fourteen seconds. In that time it increased the speed of the little ship by rather more than half a mile per second, something over 1,800 miles per hour. Before, the ship had possessed an orbital speed of a shade over 1,470 miles an hour. After the jato thrust, it was traveling nearly 3,400 miles per hour. It needed to travel something over 12,000 miles per hour to reach the artificial satellite of Earth.

The intolerable thrust ended abruptly. Joe gasped. But he could allow himself only a shake of the head to clear his brain. He jammed down the take-off rocket firing button. There was a monstrous noise and a mighty surging, and Haney panted, "Clear of cage...."

And then they were pressed fiercely against their acceleration chairs again. The ship was no longer in its launching cage. It was no longer upheld by pushpots. It was free, with its take-off rockets flaming. It plunged on up and out. But the acceleration was less. Nobody can stand six gravities for long. Anybody can take three--for a while.

Joe's body resisted movement with a weight of four hundred and fifty pounds, instead of a third as much for normal. His heart had to pump against three times the normal resistance of gravity. His chest felt as if it had a leaden weight on it. His tongue tried to crowd the back of his mouth and strangle him. The sensation was that of a nightmare of impossible duration. It was possible to move and possible to see. One could breathe, with difficulty, and with titanic effort one could speak. But there was the same feeling of stifling resistance to every movement that comes in nightmares.

But Joe managed to keep his eyes focused. The dials of the instruments said that everything was right. The tinny voice behind his head, its timbre changed by the weighting of its diaphragm, said: "***All readings check within accuracy of instruments. Good work!***"

Joe moved his eyes to a quartz window. The sky was black. But there were stars. Bright stars against a black background. At the same instant he saw the bright white disks of sunshine that came in the cabin portholes. Stars and sunshine together. And the sunshine was the sunshine of space. Even with the polarizers cutting off some of the glare it was unbearably bright and hot beyond conception. He smelled overheated paint, where the sunlight smote on a metal bulkhead. Stars and super-hot sunshine together....

It was necessary to pant for breath, and his heart pounded horribly and his eyes tried to go out of focus, but Joe Kenmore strained in his acceleration-chair and managed to laugh a little.

"We did it!" he panted. "In case you didn't notice, we're out of--the atmosphere and--out in space! We're--headed to join the Space Platform!"

2

The pressure of three gravities continued. Joe's chest muscles ached with the exertion of breathing over so long a period. Six gravities for fourteen seconds had been a ghastly ordeal. Three gravities for minutes built up to something nearly as bad. Joe's heart began to feel fatigue, and a man's heart normally simply doesn't ever feel tired. It became more and more difficult to see clearly.

But he had work to do. Important work. The take-off rockets were solid-fuel jobs, like those which launched the Platform. They were wire-wound steel tubes lined with a very special refractory, with unstable beryllium and fluorine compounds in them. The solid fuel burned at so many inches per second. The refractory crumbled away and was hurled astern at a corresponding rate--save for one small point. The refractory was not all exactly alike. Some parts of it crumbled away faster, leaving a pattern of baffles which acted like a maxim silencer on a rifle, or like an automobile muffler. The baffles set up eddies in the gas stream and produced exactly the effect of a rocket motor's throat. But the baffles themselves crumbled and were flung astern, so that the solid-fuel rockets had always the efficiency of gas-throated rocket motors; and yet every bit of refractory was reaction-mass to be hurled astern, and even the steel tubes melted and were hurled away with a gain in acceleration to the ship. Every fraction of every ounce of rocket mass was used for drive. No tanks or pumps or burners rode deadhead after they ceased to be useful.

But solid-fuel rockets simply can't be made to burn with absolute evenness as a team. Minute differences in burning-rates do tend to cancel out. But now and again they reinforce each other and if uncorrected will throw a ship off course. Gyros can't handle such effects. So Joe had to watch his instruments and listen to the tinny voice behind him and steer the ship against accidental wobblings as the Earth fell away behind him.

He battled against the fatigue of continuing to live, and struggled with gyros and steering jets to keep the ship on its hair-line course. He panted heavily. The beating of his heart became such a heavy pounding that it seemed that his whole body shook with it. He had to do infinitely fine precision steering with hands that weighed pounds and arms that weighed scores of pounds and a body that had an effective weight of almost a quarter of a ton.

And this went on and went on and on for what seemed several centuries.

Then the voice in the speaker said thickly: "*Everything is in the clear. In ten seconds you can release your rockets. Shall I count?*"

Joe panted, "Count!"

The mechanical voice said, "*Seven ... six ... five ... four ... three ... two ... one ... cut!*"

Joe pressed the release. The small, unburnt stubs of the take-off rockets went hurtling off toward emptiness. They consumed themselves as they went, and they attained an acceleration of fifty gravities once they were relieved of all load but their own substance. They had to be released lest one burn longer than another. It was also the only way to stop acceleration by solid-fuel rockets. They couldn't be extinguished. They had to be released.

From intolerably burdensome heaviness, there was abruptly no weight at all in the ship. Joe's laboring heart beat twice with the violence the weight had called for, though weight had ended. It seemed to him that his skull would crack open during those two heart-beats. Then he lay limply, resting.

There was a completely incredible stillness, for a time. The four of them panted. Haney was better off than Joe, but the Chief was harder hit. Mike's small body had taken the strain best of all, and he would use the fact later in shrill argument that midgets were designed by nature to be the explorers of space for their bulkier and less spaceworthy kindred.

The ending of the steady, punishing drag was infinitely good, but the new sensation was hardly pleasant. They had no weight. It felt as if they and the ship about them were falling together down an abyss which must have a bottom. Actually, they were falling up. But they felt a physical, crawling apprehension--a cringing from an imaginary imminent impact.

They had expected the sensation, but it was not the better for being under-stood. Joe flexed and unflexed his fingers slowly. He stirred and swallowed hastily. But the feeling persisted. He unstrapped himself from his seat. He stood up--and floated to the ceiling of the cabin. But there was of course no ceiling. Every way was up and every way was down. His stomach cramped itself in a hard knot, in the instinctive tensity of somebody in free fall.

He fended himself from the ceiling and caught at a hand-line placed there for just this necessity to grip something. In his absorption, he did not notice which way his heels went. He suddenly noticed that his companions, with regard to him, were upside down and staring at him with wooden, dazed expressions on their faces.

He tried to laugh, and gulped instead. He pulled over to the quartz-glass ports. He did not put his hand into the sunlight, but shifted the glare shutters over those ports which admitted direct sunshine. Some ports remained clear. Through one of them he saw the Earth seemingly at arm's length somewhere off. Not up, not down. Simply out from where he was. It filled all the space that the porthole showed. It was a gigantic mass of white, fleecy specks and spots which would be clouds, and between the whiteness there was a muddy dark greenish color which would be the ocean. Yet it seemed to slide very, very slowly past the window.

He saw a tanness between the clouds, and it moved inward from the edge of his field of view. He suddenly realized what it was.

"We've just about crossed the Atlantic," he said in a peculiar astonishment. But it was true the ship had not been aloft nearly as much as half an hour. "Africa's just coming into sight below. We ought to be about 1,200 miles high and still rising fast. That was the calculation."

He looked again, and then drew himself across to the opposite porthole. He saw the blackness of space, which was not blackness because it was a carpet of jewels. They were infinite in number and variations in brightness, and somehow of vastly more colorings than one noticed from Earth.

He heard the Chief grunt, and Haney gulp. He was suddenly conscious that his legs were floating rather ridiculously in mid-air with no particular relationship to anything. He saw the Chief rise very cautiously, holding on to the arms of his seat.

"Better not look at the sun," said Joe, "even though I've put on the glare-shields."

The Chief nodded. The glare-shields would keep out most of the heat and a very great deal of the ultraviolet the sun gave off. But even so, to look at the sun directly might easily result in a retinal sunburn which could result in blindness.

The loudspeaker behind Joe's chair clattered. It had seemed muted by the weight of its diaphragm at three gravities. Now it blasted unintelligibly, with no weight at all. Mike threw a switch and took the message.

"Communications says radar says we're right on course, Joe," he reported non-chalantly, "and our speed's okay. We'll reach maximum altitude in an hour and thirty-six minutes. We ought to be within calculated distance of the Platform then."

"Good," said Joe abstractedly.

He strained his eyes at the Earth. They were moving at an extraordinary speed and height. It had been reached by just four human beings before them. The tannishness which was the coast of Africa crept with astonishing slowness toward the center of what he could see.

Joe headed back to his seat. He could not walk, of course. He floated. He launched himself with a fine air of confidence. He misjudged. He was floating past his chair when he reached down--and that turned his body--and fumbled wildly. He caught hold of the back as he went by, then held on and found himself turning a grandly dignified somersault. He wound up in a remarkably foolish position with the back of his neck on the back of the chair, his arms in a highly strained position to hold him there, and his feet touching the deck of the cabin a good five feet away.

Haney looked greenish, but he said hoarsely:

"Joe, don't make me laugh--not when my stomach feels like this!"

The feeling of weightlessness was unexpectedly daunting. Joe turned himself about very slowly, with his legs floating indecorously in entirely unintended kicks. He was breathing hard when he pulled himself into the chair and strapped in once more.

"I'll take Communications," he told Mike as he settled his headphones.

Reluctantly, Mike switched over.

"Kenmore reporting to Communications," he said briefly. "We have ended our take-off acceleration. You have our course and velocity. Our instruments read--"

He went over the bank of instruments before him, giving the indication of each. In a sense, this first trip of a ship out to the Platform had some of the aspects of defusing a bomb. Calculations were useful, but observations were necessary. He had to report every detail of the condition of his ship and every instrument-reading because anything might go wrong, and at any instant. Anything that went wrong could be fatal. So every bit of data and every intended action needed to be on record. Then, if something happened, the next ship to attempt this journey might avoid the same catastrophe.

Time passed. A lot of time. The feeling of unending fall continued. They knew what it was, but they had to keep thinking of its cause to endure it. Joe found that if his mind concentrated fully on something else, it jerked back to panic and the feel of falling. But the crew of the Space Platform--now out in space for more weeks than Joe had been quarter-hours--reported that one got partly used to it, in time. When awake, at least. Asleep was another matter.

They were 1,600 miles high and still going out and up. The Earth as seen through the ports was still an utterly monstrous, bulging mass, specked with clouds above vast mottlings which were its seas and land. They might have looked for cities, but they would be mere patches in a telescope. Their task now was to wait until their orbit curved into accordance with that of the Platform and they kept their rendezvous. The artificial satellite was swinging up behind them, and was only a quarter-circle about Earth behind them. Their speed in miles per second was, at the moment, greater than that of the Platform. But they were climbing. They slowed as they climbed. When their path intersected that of the Platform, the two velocities should be exactly equal.

Major Holt's voice came on the Communicator.

"*Joe*," he said harshly, "*I have very bad news. A message came from Central Intelligence within minutes of your take-off. I--ah--with Sally I had been following your progress. I did not decode the message until now. But Central Intelligence has definite information that more than ten days ago the--ah--enemies of our Space Exploration Project--*" even on a tight beam to the small spaceship, Major Holt did not name the nation everybody knew was most desperately resolved to smash space exploration by anybody but itself--"*completed at least one rocket capable of reaching the Platform's orbit with a pay-load that could be an atomic bomb. It is believed that more than one rocket was completed. All were shipped to an unknown launching station.*"

"Not so good," said Joe.

Mike had left his post when Joe took over. Now he made a swooping dart through the air of the cabin. The midget showed no signs of the fumbling uncertainty the others had displayed--but he'd been a member of a midget acrobatic team before he went to work at the Shed. He brought himself to a stop precisely at a hand-hold, grinning triumphantly at the nearly helpless Chief and Haney.

Major Holt said in the headphones: "*It's worse than that. Radar may have told the country in question that you are on the way up. In that case, if it's even faintly possible to blast the Platform before your arrival with weapons for its defense, they'll blast.*"

"I don't like that idea," said Joe dourly. "Anything we can do?"

Major Holt laughed bitterly. "*Hardly!*" he said. "*And do you realize that if you can't unload your cargo you can't get back to Earth?*"

"Yes," said Joe. "Naturally!"

It was true. The purpose of the pushpots and the jatos and the ship's own take-off rockets had been to give it a speed at which it would inevitably rise to a height of 4,000 miles--the orbit of the Space Platform--and stay there. It would need no power to remain 4,000 miles out from Earth. But it would take power to come down. The take-off rockets had been built to drive the ship with all its contents until it attained that needed orbital velocity. There were landing rockets fastened to the hull now to slow it so that it could land. But just as the take-off rockets had been designed to lift a loaded ship, the landing-rockets had been designed to land an empty one.

The more weight the ship carried, the more power it needed to get out to the Platform. And the more power it needed to come down again.

If Joe and his companions couldn't get rid of their cargo--and they could only unload in the ship-lock of the Platform--they'd stay out in emptiness.

The Major said bitterly: "*This is all most irregular, but--here's Sally.*"

Then Sally's voice sounded in the headphones Joe wore. He was relieved that Mike wasn't acting as communications officer at the moment to overhear. But Mike was zestfully spinning like a pin-wheel in the middle of the air of the control cabin. He was showing the others that even in the intramural pastimes a spaceship crew will indulge in, a midget was better than a full-sized man. Joe said:

"Yes, Sally?"

She said unsteadily. "*I'm not going to waste your time talking to you, Joe. I think you've got to figure out something. I haven't the faintest idea what it is, but I think you can do it. Try, will you?*"

"I'm afraid we're going to have to trust to luck," admitted Joe ruefully. "We weren't equipped for anything like this."

"*No!*" said Sally fiercely. "*If I were with you, you wouldn't think of trusting to luck!*"

"I wouldn't want to," admitted Joe. "I'd feel responsible. But just the same--"

"*You're responsible now!*" said Sally, as fiercely as before. "*If the Platform's smashed, the rockets that can reach it will be duplicated to smash our cities in war! But if you can reach the Platform and arm it for defense, there won't be any war! Half the world would be praying for you, Joe, if it knew! I can't do anything else, so I'm going to start on that right now. But you try, Joe! You hear me?*"

"I'll try," said Joe humbly. "Thanks, Sally."

He heard a sound like a sob, and the headphones were silent. Joe himself swallowed very carefully. It can be alarming to be the object of an intended murder, but it can also be very thrilling. One can play up splendidly to a dramatic picture of doom. It is possible to be one's own audience and admire one's own fine disregard of danger. But when other lives depend on one, one has the irritating obligation not to strike poses but to do something practical.

Joe said somberly: "Mike, how long before we ought to contact the Platform?"

Mike reached out a small hand, caught a hand-hold, and flicked his eyes to the master chronometer.

"Forty minutes, fifty seconds. Why?"

Joe said wrily, "There are some rockets in enemy hands which can reach the Platform. They were shipped to launchers ten days ago. You figure what comes next."

Mike's wizened face became tense and angry. Haney growled, "They smash the Platform before we get to it."

"Uh-uh!" said Mike instantly. "They smash the Platform **when** we get to it! They smash us both up together. Where'll we be at contact-time, Joe?"

"Over the Indian Ocean, south of the Bay of Bengal, to be exact," said Joe.

"But we'll be moving fast. The worst of it is that it's going to take time to get in the airlock and unload our guided missiles and get them in the Platform's launching-tubes. I'd guess an hour. One bomb should get both of us above the Bay of Bengal, but we won't be set to launch a guided missile in defense until we're nearly over America again."

The Chief said sourly, "Yeah. Sitting ducks all the way across the Pacific!"

"We'll check with the Platform," said Joe. "See if you can get them direct, Mike, will you?"

Then something occurred to him. Mike scrambled back to his communication board. He began feverishly to work the computer which in turn would swing the tight-beam transmitter to the target the computer worked out, He threw a switch and said sharply, "Calling Space Platform! Pelican One calling Space Platform! Come in, Space Platform!..." He paused. "Calling Space Platform...."

Joe had a slide-rule going on another problem. He looked up, his expression peculiar.

"A solid-fuel rocket can start off at ten gravities acceleration," he said quietly, "and as its rockets burn away it can go up a lot higher than that. But 4,000 miles is a long way to go straight up. If it isn't launched yet--"

Mike snapped into a microphone: "Right!" To Joe he said, "Space Platform on the wire."

Joe heard an acknowledgment in his headphones. "I've just had word from the Shed," he explained carefully, "that there may be some guided missiles coming up from Earth to smash us as we meet. You're still higher than we are, and they ought to be starting. Can you pick up anything with your radar?"

The voice from the Platform said: "*We have picked something up. There are four rockets headed out from near the sunset-line in the Pacific. Assuming solid-fuel rockets like we used and you used, they are on a collision course.*"

"Are you doing anything about them?" asked Joe absurdly.

The voice said caustically: "*Unfortunately, we've nothing to do anything with.*" It paused. "*You, of course, can use the landing-rockets you still possess. If you fire them immediately, you will pass our scheduled meeting-place some hundreds of miles ahead of us. You will go on out to space. You may set up an orbit forty-five hundred or even five thousand miles out, and wait there for rescue.*"

Joe said briefly: "We've air for only four days. That's no good. It'll be a month before the next ship can be finished and take off. There are four rockets coming up, you say?"

"*Yes.*" The voice changed. It spoke away from the microphone. "*What's that?*" Then it returned to Joe. "*The four rockets were sent up at the same instant from four separate launching sites. Probably as many submarines at the corners of a hundred-mile square, so an accident to one wouldn't set off the others. They'll undoubtedly converge as they get nearer to us.*"

"I think," said Joe, "that we need some luck."

"*I think*," said the caustic voice, "*that we've run out of it.*"

There was a click. Joe swallowed again. The three members of his crew were looking at him.

"Somebody's fired rockets out from Earth," said Joe carefully. "They'll curve together where we meet the Platform, and get there just when we do."

The Chief rumbled. Haney clamped his jaws together. Mike's expression became one of blazing hatred.

Joe's mind went rather absurdly to the major's curious, almost despairing talk in his quarters that morning, when he'd spoken of a conspiracy to destroy all the hopes of men. The firing of rockets at the Platform was, of course, the work of men acting deliberately. But they were--unconsciously--trying to destroy their own best hopes. For freedom, certainly, whether or not they could imagine being free. But the Platform and the space exploration project in general meant benefits past computing for everybody, in time. To send ships into space for necessary but dangerous experiments with atomic energy was a purpose every man should want to help forward. To bring peace on Earth was surely an objective no man could willingly or sanely combat. And the ultimate goal of space travel was millions of other planets, circling other suns, thrown open to colonization by humanity. That prospect should surely fire every human being with enthusiasm. But something--and the more one thought about it the more specific and deliberate it seemed to be--made it necessary to fight desperately against men in order to benefit them.

Joe swallowed again. It would have been comforting to be dramatic in this war against stupidity and malice and blindness. Especially since this particular battle seemed to be lost. One could send back an eloquent, defiant message to Earth saying that the four of them did not regret their journey into space, though they were doomed to be killed by the enemies of their country. It could have been a very pretty gesture. But Joe happened to have a job to do. Pretty gestures were not a part of it. He had no idea how to do it. So he said rather sickishly:

"The Platform told me we could fire our landing-rockets as additional take-off rockets and get out of the way. Of course we've got missiles of our own on board, but we can't launch or control them. Absolutely the only thing we can choose to do or not do is fire those rockets. I'm open to suggestions if anybody can think of a way to make them useful."

There was silence. Joe's reasoning was good enough. When one can't do what he wants, one tries to make what he can do produce the results he wants. But it didn't look too promising here. They could fire the rockets now, or later, or--

An idea came out of the blue. It wasn't a good idea, but it was the only one possible under the circumstances. There was just one distinctly remote possibility. He told the others what it was. Mike's eyes flamed. The Chief nodded profoundly. Haney said with some skepticism, "It's all we've got. We've got to use it."

"I need some calculations. Spread. Best time of firing. That sort of thing. But I'm worried about calling back in the clear. A beam to the Platform will bounce and might be picked up by the enemy."

The Chief grinned suddenly. "I've got a trick for that, Joe. There's a tribesman of mine in the Shed. Get Charley Red Fox to the phone, guy, and we'll talk privately!"

The small spaceship floated on upward. It pointed steadfastly in the direction of its motion. The glaring sunshine which at its take-off had shone squarely in its bow-ports, now poured down slantingly from behind. The steel plates of the ship gleamed brightly. Below it lay the sunlit Earth. Above and about it on every hand were a multitude of stars. Even the moon was visible as the thinnest of crescents against the night of space.

The ship climbed steeply. It was meeting the Platform after only half a circuit of Earth, while the Platform had climbed upward for three full revolutions. Earth was now 3,000 miles below and appeared as the most gigantic of possible solid objects. It curved away and away to mistiness at its horizons, and it moved visibly as the spaceship floated on.

Invisible microwaves flung arrowlike through emptiness. They traveled for thousands of miles, spreading as they traveled, and then struck the strange shape of the Platform. They splashed from it. Some of them rebounded to Earth, where spies and agents of foreign powers tried desperately to make sense of the incredible syllables. They failed.

There was a relay system in operation now, from spaceship to Platform to Earth and back again. In the ship Chief Bender, Mohawk and steelman extraordinary, talked to the Shed and to one Charley Red Fox. They talked in Mohawk, which is an Algonquin Indian language, agglutinative, complicated, and not to be learned in ten easy lessons. It was not a language which eavesdroppers were likely to know as a matter of course. But it was a language by which computations could be asked for, so that a very forlorn hope might be attempted with the best possible chances of success.

Naturally, none of this appeared in the look of things. The small ship floated on and on. It reached an altitude of 3,500 miles. The Earth was visibly farther away. Behind the ship the Atlantic with its stately cloud-formations was sunlit to the very edge of its being. Ahead, the edge of night appeared beyond India. And above, the Platform appeared as a speck of molten light, quarter-illuminated by the sun above it.

Spaceship and Platform moved on toward a meeting place. The ship moved a trifle faster, because it was climbing. The speeds would match exactly when they met. The small torpedo-shaped shining ship and the bulging glowing metal satellite floated with a seeming vast deliberation in emptiness, while the most gigantic of possible round objects filled all the firmament beneath them. They were 200 miles apart. It seemed that the huge Platform overtook the shining ship. It did. They were only 50 miles apart and still closing in.

By that time the twilight band of Earth's surface was nearly at the center of the planet, and night filled more than a quarter of its disk.

By that time, too, even to the naked eye through the ports of the supply-ship the enemy rockets had become visible. They were a thin skein of threads of white vapor which seemed to unravel in nothingness. The vapor curled and expanded preposterously. It could just be seen to be jetting into existence from four separate points, two a little ahead of the others. They came out from Earth at a rate which seemed remarkably deliberate until one saw with what fury the rocket-fumes spat out to form the whitish threads. Then one could guess at a three-or even four-stage launching series, so that what appeared to be mere pinpoints would really be rockets carrying half-ton atomic warheads with an attained velocity of 10,000 miles per hour and more straight up.

The threads unraveled in a straight line aimed at the two metal things floating in emptiness. One was small and streamlined, with inadequate landing-rockets clamped to its body and with stubby fins that had no possible utility out of air. The other was large and clumsy to look at, but very, very stately indeed in its progress through the heavens. They floated smoothly toward a rendezvous. The rockets from Earth came ravening to destroy them at the instant of their intersection.

The little spaceship turned slowly. Its rounded bow had pointed longingly at the stars. Now it tilted downward. Its direction of movement did not change, of course. In the absence of air, it could tumble indefinitely without any ill effect. It was in a trajectory instead of on a course, though presently the trajectory would become an orbit. But it pointed nose-down toward the Earth even as it continued to hurtle onward.

The great steel hull and the small spaceship were 20 miles apart. An infinitesimal radar-bowl moved on the little ship. Tight-beam waves flickered invisibly between the two craft. The rockets raged toward them.

The ship and the Platform were 10 miles apart. The rockets were now glinting missiles leaping ahead of the fumes that propelled them.

The ship and the Platform were two miles apart. The rockets rushed upward.... There were minute corrections in their courses. They converged....

Flames leaped from the tiny ship. Its landing-rockets spouted white-hot flame and fumes more thick and coiling than even the smoke of the bombs. The little ship surged momentarily toward the racing monsters. And then----

The rockets which were supposed to let the ship down to Earth flew free--flung themselves unburdened at the rockets which came with deadly intent to the meeting of the two Earth spacecraft.

The landing-rockets plunged down at forty gravities or better. They were a dwindling group of infinitely bright sparks which seemed to group themselves more closely as they dwindled. They charged upon the attacking robot things. They were unguided, of necessity, but the robot bombs had to be equipped with proximity fuses. No remote control could be so accurate as to determine the best moment for detonation at 4,000 miles' distance. So the war rockets had to be devised to explode when near anything which reflected their probing radar waves. They had to be designed to be triggered by anything in space.

And the loosed landing-rockets plunged among them.

They did not detonate all at once. That was mathematically impossible. But no human eye could detect the delay. Four close-packed flares of pure atomic fire sprang into being between the Platform and Earth. Each was brighter than the sun. For the fraction of an instant there was no night where night had fallen on the Earth. For thousands of miles the Earth glowed brightly.

Then there was a twisting, coiling tumult of incandescent gases, which were snatched away by nothingness and ceased to be.

Then there were just two things remaining in the void. One was the great, clumsy, shining Platform, gigantic in size to anything close by. The other was the small spaceship which had climbed to it and fought for it and defended it against the bombs from Earth.

The little ship now had a slight motion away from the Platform, due to the instant's tugging by its rockets before they were released.

It turned about in emptiness. Its steering-rockets spouted smoke. It began to cancel out its velocity away from the Platform, and to swim slowly and very carefully toward it.

3

Making actual contact with the platform was not a matter for instruments and calculations. It had to be done directly--by hand, as it were. Joe watched out the ports and played the controls of the steering jets with a nerve-racked precision. His task was not easy.

Before he could return to the point of rendezvous, the blinding sunlight on the Platform took on a tinge of red. It was the twilight-zone of the satellite's orbit, when for a time the sunlight that reached it was light which had passed through Earth's atmosphere and been bent by it and colored crimson by the dust in Earth's air. It glowed a fiery red, and the color deepened, and then there was darkness.

They were in Earth's shadow. There were stars to be seen, but no sun. The Moon was hidden, too. And the Earth was a monstrous, incredible, abysmal blackness which at this first experience of its appearance produced an almost superstitious terror. Formerly it had seemed a distant but sunlit world, flecked with white clouds and with sprawling differentiations of color beneath them.

Now it did not look like a solid thing at all. It looked like a hole in creation. One could see ten thousand million stars of every imaginable tint and shade. But where the Earth should be there seemed a vast nothingness. It looked like an opening to annihilation. It looked like the veritable Pit of Darkness which is the greatest horror men have ever imagined, and since those in the ship were without weight it seemed that they were falling into it.

Joe knew better, of course. So did the others. But that was the look of things, and that was the feeling. One did not feel in danger of death, but of extinction--which, in cold fact, is very much worse.

Lights glowed on the outside of the Platform to guide the supply ship to it. There were red and green and blue and harsh blue-white electric bulbs. They were bright and distinct, but the feeling of loneliness above that awful appearance of the Pit was appalling. No small child alone at night had ever so desolate a sensation of isolation as the four in the small ship.

But Joe painstakingly played the buttons of the steering-rocket control board. The ship surged, and turned, and surged forward again. Mike, at the communicator, said, "They say slow up, Joe."

Joe obeyed, but he was tense. Haney and the Chief were at other portholes, looking out. The Chief said heavily, "Fellas, I'm going to admit I never felt so lonesome in my life!"

"I'm glad I've got you fellows with me!" Haney admitted guiltily.

"The job's almost over," said Joe.

The ship's own hull, outside the ports, glowed suddenly in a light-beam from the Platform. The small, brief surges of acceleration which sent the ship on produced tremendous emotional effects. When the Platform was only one mile away, Haney switched on the ship's searchlights. They stabbed through emptiness with absolutely no sign of their existence until they touched the steel hull of the satellite.

Mike said sharply: "Slow up some more, Joe."

He obeyed again. It would not be a good idea to ram the Platform after they had come so far to reach it.

They drifted slowly, slowly, slowly toward it. The monstrous Pit of Darkness which was the night side of Earth seemed almost about to engulf the Platform. They were a few hundred feet higher than the great metal globe, and the blackness was behind it. They were a quarter of a mile away. The distance diminished.

A thin straight line seemed to grow out toward them. There was a small, bulb-like object at its end. It reached out farther than was at all plausible. Nothing so slender should conceivably reach so far without bending of its own weight. But of course it had no weight here. It was a plastic flexible hose with air pressure in it. It groped for the spaceship.

The four in the ship held their breaths.

There was a loud, metallic *clank!*

Then it was possible to feel the ship being pulled toward the Platform by the magnetic grapple. It was a landing-line. It was the means by which the ship would be docked in the giant lock which had been built to receive it.

As they drew near, they saw the joints of the plating of the Platform. They saw rivets. There was the huge, 30-foot doorway with its valves swung wide. Their searchlight beam glared into it. They saw the metal floor, and the bulging plastic sidewalls, restrained by nets. They saw the inner lock-door. It seemed that men should be visible to welcome them. There were none.

The airlock swallowed them. They touched against something solid. There were more clankings. They seemed to crunch against the metal floor--magnetic flooring-grapples. Then, in solid contact with the substance of the Platform, they heard the sounds of the great outer doors swinging shut. They were within the artificial satellite of Earth. It was bright in the lock, and Joe stared out the cabin ports at the quilted sides. There was a hissing of air, and he saw a swirling mist, and then the bulges of the sidewall sagged. The air pressure gauge was spinning up toward normal sea-level air pressure.

Joe threw the ready lever of the steering rockets to *Off.* "We're landed."

There was silence. Joe looked about him. The other three looked queer. It would have seemed natural for them to rejoice on arriving at their destination. But somehow they didn't feel that they had.

Joe said wrily, "It seems that we ought to weigh something, now we've got here. So we feel queer that we don't. Shoes, Mike?"

Mike peeled off the magnetic-soled slippers from their place on the cabin wall. He handed them out and opened the door. A biting chill came in it. Joe slipped on the shoe-soles with their elastic bands to hold them. He stepped out the door.

He didn't land. He floated until he reached the sidewall. Then he pulled himself down by the netting. Once he touched the floor, his shoes seemed to be sticky. The net and the plastic sidewalls were, of course, the method by which a really large airlock was made practical. When this ship was about to take off again, pumps would not labor for hours to pump the air out. The sidewalls would inflate and closely enclose the ship's hull, and so force the air in the lock back into the ship. Then the pumps would work on the air behind the inflated walls--with nets to help them draw the wall-stuff back to let the ship go free. The lock could be used with only fifteen minutes for pumping instead of four hours.

The door in the back of the lock clanked open. Joe tried to walk toward it. He discovered his astounding clumsiness. To walk in magnetic-soled shoes in weightlessness requires a knack. When Joe lifted one foot and tried to swing the other forward, his body tried to pivot. When he lifted his right foot, he had to turn his left slightly inward. His arms tried to float absurdly upward. When he was in motion and essayed to pause, his whole body tended to continue forward with a sedate toppling motion that brought him down flat on his face. He had to put one foot forward to check himself. He seemed to have no sense of balance. When he stood still--his stomach queasy because of weightlessness--he found himself tilting undignifiedly forward or back--or, with equal unpredictability, sidewise. He would have to learn an entirely new method of walking.

A man came in the lock, and Joe knew who it was. Sanford, the senior scientist of the Platform's crew. Joe had seen him often enough on the television screen in the Communications Room at the Shed. Now Sanford looked nerve-racked, but his eyes were bright and his expression sardonic.

"My compliments," he said, his voice tight with irony, "for a splendidly futile job well done! You've got your cargo invoice?"

Joe nodded. Sanford held out his hand. Joe fumbled in his pocket and brought out the yellow sheet.

"I'd like to introduce my crew," said Joe. "This is Haney, and Chief Bender, and Mike Scandia." He waved his hand, and his whole body wobbled unexpectedly.

"We'll know each other!" said Sanford sardonically. "Our first job is more futility--to get the guided missiles you've brought us into the launching tubes. A lot of good they'll do!"

A huge plate in the roof of the lock--but it was not up or down or in any particular direction--withdrew itself. A man floated through the opening and landed on the ship's hull; another man followed him.

"Chief," said Joe, "and Haney. Will you open the cargo doors?"

The two swaying figures moved to obey, though with erratic clumsiness. Sanford called sharply: "Don't touch the hull without gloves! If it isn't nearly red-hot from the sunlight, it'll be below zero from shadow!"

Joe realized, then, the temperature effects the skin on his face noticed. A part of the spaceship's hull gave off heat like that of a panel heating installation. Another part imparted a chill.

Sanford said unpleasantly, "You want to report your heroism, eh? Come along!"

He clanked to the doorway by which he had entered. Joe followed, and Mike after him.

They went out of the lock. Sanford suddenly peeled off his metal-soled slippers, put them in his pocket, and dived casually into a four-foot metal tube. He drifted smoothly away along the lighted bore, not touching the sidewalls. He moved in the manner of a dream, when one floats with infinite ease and precision in any direction one chooses.

Joe and Mike did not share his talent. Joe launched himself after Sanford, and for perhaps 20 or 30 feet the lighted aluminum sidewall of the tube sped past him. Then his shoulder rubbed, and he found himself skidding to an undignified stop, choking the bore. Mike thudded into him.

"I haven't got the hang of this yet," said Joe apologetically.

He untangled himself and went on. Mike followed him, his expression that of pure bliss. He was a tiny man, was Mike, but he had the longings and the ambitions of half a dozen ordinary-sized men in his small body. And he had known frustration. He could prove by mathematics that space exploration could be carried on by midgets at a fraction of the cost and risk of the same job done by normal-sized men. He was, of course, quite right. The cabins and air and food supplies for a spaceship's crew of midgets would cost and weigh a fraction of similar equipment for six-footers. But people simply weren't interested in sending midgets out into space.

But Mike had gotten here. He was in the Space Platform. There were full-sized men who would joyfully have changed places with him, forty-one inch height and all. So Mike was blissful.

The tube ended and Joe bounced off the wall that faced its end. Sanford was waiting. He grinned with more than a hint of spite.

"Here's our communications room," he said. "Now you can talk down to Earth. It'll be relayed, now, but in half an hour you can reach the Shed direct."

He floated inside. Joe followed cautiously. There was another crew member on duty there. He sat before a group of radar screens, with thigh grips across his legs to hold him in his chair. He turned his head and nodded cheerfully enough.

"Here!" snapped Sanford.

Joe clambered awkwardly to the seat the senior crew member pointed out. He made his way to it by handholds on the walls. He fumbled into the chair and threw over the curved thigh grips that would hold him in place.

Suddenly he was oriented. He had seen this room before--before the Platform was launched. True, the man at the radar screens was upside-down with reference to himself, and Sanford had hooked a knee negligently around the arm of a firmly anchored chair with his body at right angles to Joe's own, but at least Joe knew where he was and what he was to do.

"Go ahead and report," said Sanford sardonically. "You might tell them that you heroically destroyed the rockets that attacked us, and that your crew behaved splendidly, and that you have landed in the Space Platform and the situation is well in hand. It isn't, but it will make nice headlines."

Joe said evenly, "Our arrival's been reported?"

"No," said Sanford, grinning. "Obviously the radar down on Earth--shipboard ones on this hemisphere, of course--have reported that the Platform still exists. But we haven't communicated since the bombs went off. They probably think we had so many punctures that we lost all our air and are all wiped out. They'll be glad to hear from you that we aren't."

Joe threw a switch, frowning. This wasn't right. Sanford was the senior scientist on board and hence in command, because he was best-qualified to direct the scientific observations the Platform was making. But there was something specifically wrong.

The communicator hummed. A faint voice sounded. It swelled to loudness. "Calling Space Platform! *Calling Space Platform!* CALLING SPACE PLATFORM!" Joe turned down the volume. He said into the microphone:

"Space Platform calling Earth. Joe Kenmore reporting. We have made contact with the Platform and completed our landing. Our cargo is now being unloaded. Our landing rockets had to be expended against presumably hostile bombs, and we are now unable to return to Earth. The ship and the Platform, however, are unharmed. I am now waiting for orders. Report ends."

He turned away from the microphone. Sanford said sharply, "Go on! Tell them what a hero you are!"

"I'm going to help unload my ship," Joe said shortly. "You report what you please."

"Get back at that transmitter!" shouted Sanford furiously. "Tell 'em you're a hero! Tell 'em you're wonderful! I'll tell 'em how useless it is!"

Joe saw the other man in the room, the man at the radar screens, shake his head. He got up and fumbled his way along the wall to the door. Sanford shouted after him angrily.

Joe went out, found the four-foot tunnel, and floated not down but along it back to the unloading lock. Wordlessly, he set to work to get the cargo out of the cargo hold of the spaceship.

Handling objects in weightlessness which on Earth would be heavy was an art in itself. Two men could move tons. It needed only one man to start a massive crate in motion. However, one had either to lift or push an object in the exact line it was to follow. To thrust hard for a short time produced exactly the same effect as to push gently for a longer period. Anything floated tranquilly in the line along which it was moved. The man who had to stop it, though, needed to use exactly as much energy as the man who sent it floating. He needed to check the floating thing in exactly the same line. If one tried to stop a massive shipment from one side, he would topple into it and he and the crate together would go floundering helplessly over each other.

The Chief had gone off to help maneuver two-ton guided missiles into launching tubes. One crew member remained with Haney, unloading things that would have had to be handled with cranes on Earth. Joe found himself needed most in the storage chamber. A crate floated from the ship to the crewman. Standing head downward, he stopped its original movement, braced himself, and sent it floating to Joe. He braced himself, stopped its flight, and very slowly--to move fast with anything heavy in his hands would pull his feet from the floor--set it on a stack of similar objects which would presently be fastened in place.

Everything had to be done in slow motion, or one would lose his footing. Joe worked painstakingly. He gradually began to understand the process. But the muscles of his stomach ached because of their continuous, instinctive cramp due to the sensation of unending fall.

Mike floated through the hatchway from the lock. He twisted about as he floated, and his magnetized soles clanked to a deft contact with the wall. He said calmly: "That guy Sanford has cracked up. He's potty. If this were jail he'd be stir-crazy. He's yelling into the communicator now that we'll all be dead in a matter of days, and the rocket missiles we brought up won't help. He's nasty about it, too!"

Haney called from the cargo space of the ship in the lock: "All empty here! We're unloaded."

There were sounds as he closed the cargo doors. Haney, followed by the Chief, came into view, floating as Mike had done. But he didn't land as skillfully. He touched the wall on his hands and knees and bounced away and tried helplessly to swim to a hand-hold. It would have been funny except that Joe was in no mood for humor.

Mike whipped off his belt and flipped the end of it to Haney. He caught it and was drawn gently to the wall. Haney's shoes clicked to a hold. The Chief landed more expertly.

"We need wings here," he said ruefully. "You reported, Joe?"

Joe nodded. He turned to Brent, the crew member who'd been unloading. He knew him too, from their two-way video conversations.

"Sanford does act oddly," he said uncomfortably. "When he met me in the lock he said our coming was useless. He talked about the futility of everything while I reported. He sounds like he sneers at every possible action as useless."

"Most likely it is," Brent said mildly. "Here, anyhow. It does look as if we're going to be knocked off. But Sanford's taking it badly. The rest of us have let him act as he pleased because it didn't seem to matter. It probably doesn't, except that he's annoying."

Mike said truculently, "We won't be knocked off! We've got rockets of our own up here now! We can fight back if there's another attack!"

Brent shrugged. His face was young enough, but deeply lined. He said as mildly as before: "Your landing rockets set off four bombs on the way from Earth. You brought us six more rocket missiles. How many bombs can we knock down with them?"

Joe blinked. It was a shock to realize the facts of life in an artificial satellite. If it could be reached by bombs from Earth, the bombs could be reached by guided missiles from the satellite. But it would take one guided missile to knock down one bomb--with luck.

"I see," said Joe slowly. "We can handle just six more bombs from Earth."

"Six in the next month," agreed Brent wrily. "It'll be that long before we get more. Somebody sent up four bombs today. Suppose they send eight next time? Or simply one a day for a week?"

Mike made an angry noise. "The seventh bomb shot at us knocks us out! We're sitting ducks here too!"

Brent nodded. He said mildly:

"Yes. The Platform can't be defended against an indefinite number of bombs from Earth. Of course the United States could go to war because we've been shot at. But would that do us any good? We'd be shot down in the war."

Joe said distastefully, "And Sanford's cracked up because he knows he's going to be killed?"

Brent said earnestly. "Oh, no! He's a good scientist! But he's always had a brilliant mind. Poor devil, he's never failed at anything in all his life until now! Now he *has* failed. He's going to be killed, and he can't think of any way to stop it. His brains are the only things he's ever believed in, and now they're no good. He can't accept the idea that he's stupid, so he has to believe that everything else is. It's a necessity for him. Haven't you known people who had to think everybody else was stupid to keep from knowing that they were themselves?"

Joe nodded. He waited.

"Sanford," said Brent earnestly, "simply can't adjust to the discovery that he's no better than anybody else. That's all. He was a nice guy, but he's not used to frustration and he can't take it. Therefore he scorns everything that frustrates him--and everything else, by necessity. He'll be scornful about getting killed when it happens. But waiting for it is becoming intolerable to him."

He looked at his watch. He said apologetically, "I'm the crew psychologist. That's why I speak so firmly. In five minutes we're due to come out of the Earth's shadow into sunshine again. I'd suggest that you come to watch. It's good to look at."

He did not wait for an answer. He led the way. And the others followed in a strange procession. Somehow, automatically, they fell into single file, and they moved on their magnetic-soled slippers toward a passage tube in one wall. Their slipper soles clanked and clicked in an erratic rhythm. Brent walked with the mincing steps necessary for movement in weightlessness. The others imitated him. Their hands no longer hung naturally by their sides, but tended to make extravagant gestures with the slightest muscular impulse. They swayed extraordinarily as they walked. Brent was a slender figure, and Joe was more thick-set, and Haney was taller, and lean. The burly Chief and the forty-one inch figure of Mike the midget followed after them. They made a queer procession indeed.

Minutes later they were in a blister on the skin of the Platform. There were quartz glass ports in the sidewall. Outside the glass were metal shutters. Brent served out dense goggles, almost black, and touched the buttons that opened the steel port coverings.

They looked into space. The dimmer stars were extinguished by the goggles they wore. The brighter ones seemed faint and widely spaced. Beneath their feet as they held to handrails lay the featureless darkness of Earth. But before them and very far away there was a vast, dim arch of deepest red.

It was sunlight filtered through the thickest layers of Earth's air. It barely outlined the curve of that gigantic globe. As they stared, it grew brighter. The artificial satellite required little more than four hours for one revolution about its primary, the Earth. To those aboard it, the Earth would go through all its phases in no longer a time. They saw now the thinnest possible crescent of the new Earth. But in minutes--almost in seconds--the deep red sunshine brightened to gold. The hair-thin line of light widened to a narrow ribbon which described an eight-thousand-mile half-circle. It brightened markedly at the middle. It remained red at its ends, but in the very center it glowed with splendid flame. Then a golden ball appeared, and swam up and detached itself from the Earth, and the on-lookers saw the breath-taking spectacle of all of Earth's surface seemingly being born of the night.

As if new-created before their eyes, seas and lands unfolded in the sunlight. They watched flecks of cloud and the long shadows of mountains, and the strangely different colorings of its fields and forests.

As Brent had told them, it was good to watch.

It was half an hour later when they gathered in the kitchen of the Platform. The man who had been loading launching tubes now briskly worked to prepare a meal on the extremely unusual cooking-devices of a human outpost in interplanetary space.

The food smelled good. But Joe noticed that he could smell growing things. Green stuff. It was absurd--until he remembered that there was a hydroponic garden here. Plants grew in it under sunlamps which were turned on for a certain number of hours every day. The plants purified the Platform's air, and of course provided some fresh and nourishing food for the crew.

They ate. The food was served in plastic bowls, with elastic thread covers through which they could see and choose the particular morsels they fancied next. The threads stretched to let through the forks they ate with. But Brent used a rather more practical pair of tongs in a businesslike manner.

They drank coffee from cups which looked very much like ordinary cups on Earth. Joe remembered suddenly that Sally Holt had had much to do with the design of domestic science arrangements here. He regarded his cup with interest. It stayed in its saucer because of magnets in both plastic articles. The saucer stayed on the table because the table was magnetic, too. And the coffee did not float out to mid-air in a hot, round brownish ball, because there was a transparent cover over the cup. When one put his lips to the proper edge, a part of the cover yielded as the cup was squeezed. The far side of the cup was flexible. One pressed, and the coffee came into one's lips without the spilling of a drop.

At that moment Joe really thought of Sally for the first time in a good two hours. She'd been anxious that living in the Platform should be as normal and Earth-like as possible. The total absence of weight would be bad enough. She believed it needed to be countered, as a psychological factor in staying sane, by the effect of normal-seeming chairs and normal-tasting food, and not too exotic systems for eating.

Joe asked Brent about it.

"Oh, yes," said Brent mildly. "It's likely we'd all have gone off the deep end if there weren't some familiar things about. To have to drink from a cup that one squeezes is tolerable. But we'd have felt hysterical at times if we had to drink everything from the equivalent of baby bottles."

"Sally Holt," said Joe, "is a friend of mine. She helped design this stuff."

"That girl has every ounce of brains that any woman can be trusted with!" Brent said warmly. "She thought of things that would never have occurred to me! As a psychologist, I could see how good her ideas were when she brought them up, but as a male I'd never have dreamed of them." Then he grinned. "She fell down on just one point. So did everybody else. Nobody happened to think of a garbage-disposal system for the Platform."

It came into Joe's mind that garbage-disposal was hardly a subject one would expect to be discussing in interplanetary space. But the Platform wasn't the same thing as a spaceship. A ship could jettison refuse and leave it behind, or store it during a voyage and dump it at either end. But the Space Platform would never land. It could roll on forever. And if it heaved out its refuse from airlocks--why--the stuff would still have the Platform's orbital speed and would follow it tirelessly around the Earth until the end of time.

"We dry and store it now," said Brent. "If we were going to live, we'd figure out some way to turn it to fertilizer for the hydroponic gardens. It's hardly worth while as things are. Even then, though, the problem of tin cans could be hopeless."

The Chief wiped his mouth deliberately. He had helped load four guided-missile launching tubes, and he had been brought up to date on the state of things in the Platform. He growled in a preliminary fashion and said, "Joe."

Joe looked at him.

"We brought up six two-ton guided missiles," said the Chief dourly. "We'll have warning of other bombs coming up. We can send these missiles out to intercept 'em. Six of 'em. They can get close enough to set off their proximity fuses, anyhow. But what are we going to do, Joe, if somebody flings seven bombs at us? We can manage six--maybe. But what'll we do with the one that's left over?"

"Have you any ideas?" asked Joe.

The Chief shook his head. Brent said mildly. "We've worked on that here in the Platform, I assure you. And as Sanford puts it quite soundly, about the only thing we can really do is throw our empty tin cans at them."

Joe nodded. Then he tensed. Brent had meant it as a rather mirthless joke. But Joe was astonished at what his own brain made of it. He thought it over. Then he said, "Why not? It ought to be a very good trick."

Brent stared at him incredulously. Haney looked solemnly at him. The Chief regarded Joe thoughtfully out of the corner of his eye. Then Mike shouted gleefully. The Chief blinked, and a moment later grunted wrathful unintelligible syllables of Mohawk, and then tried to pound Joe on the back and because of his want of weight went head over heels into the air between the six walls of the kitchen.

Haney said disgustedly, "Joe, there are times when a guy wants to murder you! Why didn't I think of that?"

But Brent was looking at the four of them with a lively, helpless curiosity. "Will you guys let me in on this?"

They told him. Joe began to explain it carefully, but the Chief broke in with a barked and impatient description, and then Mike interrupted to snap a correction. But by that time Brent's expression had changed with astonishing suddenness.

"I see! I see!" he said excitedly. "All right! Have you got space suits in your ship? We have them. So we'll go out and pelt the stars with garbage. I think we'd better get at it right now, too. In under two hours we'll be a fine target for more bombs, and it would be good to start ahead of time."

Mike made a gesture and went floating out of the kitchen, air-swimming to go get space suits from the ship. The grin on his small face threatened to cut his throat. Joe asked, "Sanford's in command. How'll he like this idea?"

Brent hesitated. "I'm afraid," he said regretfully, "he won't like it. If you solve a problem he gave up, it will tear his present adjustment to bits. He's gone psychotic. I think, though, that he'll allow it to be tried while he swears at us for fools. He's most likely to react that way if you suggest it."

"Then," agreed Joe, "I suggest it. Chief----"

The Chief raised a large brown hand.

"I got the program, Joe," he said. "We'll all get set."

And Joe went floating unhappily through passage-tubes to the control room. He heard Sanford's voice, sardonic and mocking, as he reached the communications room door.

"What do you expect?" Sanford was saying derisively. "We're clay pigeons. We're a perfect target. We've just so much ammunition now. You say you may send us more in three weeks instead of a month. I admire your persistence, but it's really no use! This is all a very stupid business...."

He felt Joe's presence. He turned, and then sharply struck the communicator switch with the heel of his hand. The image on the television screen died. The voice cut off. He said blandly: "Well?"

"I want," said Joe, "to take a garbage-disposal party out on the outside of the Platform. I came to ask for authority."

Sanford looked at him in mocking surprise.

"To be sure it seems as intelligent as anything else the human race has ever done," he observed. "But why does it appeal to you as something you want to do?"

"I think," Joe told him, "that we can make a defense against bombs from Earth with our empty tin cans."

Sanford raised his eyebrows.

"If you happen to have a four-leaf clover with you," he said in fine irony, "I'm told they're good, too."

His eyes were bright and scornful. His manner was feverishly derisive. Joe would have done well to let it go at that. But he was nettled.

"We set off the last bombs," he said doggedly, "by shooting our landing rockets at them. They didn't collide with the bombs. They simply touched off the bombs' proximity fuses. If we surround the Platform with a cluster of tin cans and such things, they may do as well. Things we throw away won't drop to Earth. Ultimately, they'll actually circle us, like satellites themselves. But if we can get enough of them between us and Earth, any bombs that come up will have their proximity fuses detonated by the floating trash we throw out."

Sanford laughed.

"We might ask for aluminum-foil ribbon to come up in the next supply ship," said Joe. "We could have masses of that, or maybe metallic dust floating around us."

"I much prefer used tin cans," said Sanford humorously. "I'll take the watch here and let everybody go out with you. By all means we must defend ourselves. Forward with the garbage! Go ahead!"

His eyes were almost hysterically scornful as he waited for Joe to leave. Joe did not like it at all, but there was nothing to do but get out.

He found the Chief with a net bag filled with emptied tin cans. Haney had another. There were two more, carried by members of the Platform's four-man crew. They were donning their space suits when Joe came upon them. Mike was grotesque in the cut-down outfit built for him. Actually, the only difference was in the size of the fabric suit and the length of the arms and legs. He could carry a talkie outfit with its batteries, and the oxygen tank for breathing as well as anybody, since out here weight did not count at all. There were plastic ropes, resistant to extremes of temperature.

Joe got into his own space suit. It was no such self-contained space craft in itself as the fantastic story tellers dreamed of. It was not much more than an altitude suit, aluminized to withstand the blazing heat of sunshine in emptiness, and with extravagantly insulated soles to the magnetic boots. In theory, there simply is no temperature in space. In practice, a metal hull heats up in sunshine to very much more than any record-hot-day temperature on Earth. In shadow, too, a metal hull will drop very close to minus 250 degrees Centigrade, which is something like 400 degrees Fahrenheit below zero. But mainly the space boots were insulated against the almost dull-red-heat temperatures of long-continued sunshine.

A crewman named Corey moved into an airlock with one of the bags of empty tin cans. Brent watched in a routine fashion through a glass in the lock-door. The pumps began to exhaust the air from the airlock. Corey's space suit inflated visibly. Presently the pump stopped. Corey opened the outer door. He went out, paying plastic rope behind him. An instant later he reappeared and removed the rope. He'd made his line fast outside. He closed the outer lock-door. Air surged into the lock and Haney crowded in. Again the pumping. Then Haney went out, and was anchored to the Platform not only by his magnetic boots but by a rope fastened to a hand-hold. Brent went out. Mike. Joe came next.

They stood on the hull of the Space Platform, waiting in the incredible harsh sunshine of emptiness. The bright steel plates of the hull swelled and curved away on every hand. There were myriads of stars and the vast round bulk of Earth seemed farther away to a man in a space suit than to a man looking out a port. Where shadows cut across the Platform's irregular surface, there was utter blackness. Also there was horrible frigidity. Elsewhere it was blindingly bright. The men were specks of humanity standing on a shining metal hull, and all about them there was the desolation of nothingness.

But Joe felt strangely proud. The seventh man came out of the lock-door. They tied their plastic ropes together and spread out in a long line which went almost around the Platform. The man next to the lock was anchored to a steel hand-hold. The third man of the line also anchored himself. The fifth. The seventh. They were a straggling line of figures with impossibly elongated shadows, held together by ropes. They were peculiarly like a party of weirdly costumed mountaineers on a glacier of gleaming silver.

But no mountain climbers ever had a background of ten thousand million stars, peering up from below them as well as from overhead. Nor did any ever have a mottled greenish planet rolling by 4,000 miles beneath them, nor a blazing sun glaring down at them from a sky such as this.

In particular, perhaps, no other explorers ever set out upon an expedition whose purpose was to throw tin cans and dried refuse at all the shining cosmos.

They set to work. The space suits were inevitably clumsy. It was not easy to throw hard with only magnetism to hold one to his feet. It was actually more practical to throw straight up with an underhand gesture. But even that would send the tin cans an enormous distance, in time. There was no air to slow them.

The tin cans twinkled as they left the Platform's steel expanse. They moved away at a speed of possibly 20 to 30 miles an hour. They floated off in all possible directions. They would never reach Earth, of course. They shared the Platform's orbital speed, and they would circle the Earth with it forever. But when they were thrown away, their orbits were displaced a little. Each can thrown downward just now, for example, would always be between the Platform and the Earth on this side of its orbit. But on the other side of Earth it would be above the Platform. The Platform, in fact, became the center of a swarm, a cluster, a cloud of infinitesimal objects which would always accompany it and always be in motion with regard to it. Together, they should make up a screen no proximity fuse bomb could pierce without exploding.

Joe heard clankings, transmitted to his body through his feet.

"What's that?" he demanded sharply. "It sounds like the airlock!"

Voices mingled in his ears. The other walkie-talkies allowed everybody to speak at once. Most of them did. Then Joe heard someone laugh. It was Sanford's voice.

Sandford's aluminized, space-suited figure came clanking around the curve of the small metal world. The antenna of his walkie-talkie glittered above his head. He seemed to swagger against the background of many-colored stars.

Brent spoke quickly, before anyone else could question Sanford. His tone was mild and matter of fact, but Joe somehow knew the tension behind it.

"Hello, Sanford. You came out? Was it wise? Shouldn't there be someone inside the Platform?"

Sanford laughed again. "It was very wise. We're going to be killed, as you fellows know perfectly well. It's futile to try to avoid it. So very sensibly I've decided to spare myself the nuisance of waiting to be killed. I came out."

There was silence in the ear-phones of Joe's space suit radio. He heard his own heart beating loudly and steadily in the absolute stillness.

"Incidentally," said Sanford with almost hysterical amusement, "I fixed it so that none of us can get back in. It would be useless, anyhow. Everything's futility. So I've put an end to our troubles for good. I've locked us all out."

He laughed yet again. And Joe knew that in Sanford's madness it was perfectly possible for him to have done exactly what he said.

There were eight human beings on the Platform. All were now outside it, on its outer skin. They wore space suits with from half an hour to an hour's oxygen supply. They had no tools with which to break back into the satellite. And no help could possibly reach them in less than three weeks.

If they couldn't get back inside the Platform, Sanford, laughing proudly, had killed them all.

4

There was a babbling of angry, strained, tense voices in Joe's headphones. Then the Chief roared for silence. It fell, save for Sanford's quiet, hysterical chuckling. Joe found himself rather absurdly thinking that Sanford was not actually insane, except as any man may be who believes only in his own cleverness. Sooner or later it is bound to fail him. On Earth, Sanford's pride in his own intellect had been useful. He had been brilliant because he accepted every problem and every difficulty as a challenge. But with the Platform's situation seemingly hopeless, he'd been starkly unable to face the fact that he wasn't clever or brilliant or intelligent enough. If Joe's solution to the proximity fuse bombs had been offered before his emotional collapse, he could have accepted it grandly, and in so doing have made it his own. But it was too late for that now. He'd given up and worked up a frantic scorn for the universe he could not cope with. For Joe's trick to work would have made him inferior even to Joe in his own view. And he couldn't have that! Even to die, with the prospect that others would survive him, was an intolerable prospect. He had to be smarter than anybody else.

So he chuckled. The Chief roared wrathfully into his transmitter: "Quiet! This crazy fool's tried to commit suicide for all of us! How about it? Why can't we get back in? How many locks----"

Joe found himself thinking hard. He could be angry later. Now there wasn't time. Thirty or forty minutes of breathing. No tools. A steel hull. The airlocks were naturally arranged for the greatest possible safety under normal conditions. In every airlock it had naturally been arranged so that the door to space and the door to the interior could not be open at the same time. That was to save lives. To save air, it would naturally be arranged that the door to space couldn't be opened until the lock was pumped empty.

That in itself could be an answer. Joe said sharply, "Hold it, Chief! Somebody watch Sanford! All we've got to do is find which lock he came out of. He couldn't get out until he pumped it empty--and that unlocks the outer door!"

But Sanford laughed once more. He sounded like someone in the highest of high good humor.

"Heroic again, eh? But I took a compressed air bottle in the lock with me. When the outer door was open, I opened the stopcock and shut the door. The air bottle filled the lock behind me. Naturally I'd fasten the door after I came out! One must be intelligent!"

Joe heard Brent muttering, "Yes, he'd do that!"

"Somebody check it!" snapped Joe. "Make sure! It might amuse him to watch us die while he knew we could get back in if we were as smart as he is."

There were clankings on the hull. Men moved, unfastening the lines which held them to the hull to get freedom of movement, but not breaking the links which bound them to each other. Joe saw Haney go grimly back to the task of throwing away the stuff that they had brought out for the purpose. Then Mike's voice, brittle and cagey: "Haney! Quit it!"

Sanford's voice again, horribly amused. "By all means! Don't throw away our garbage! We may need it!"

A voice snapped, "This lock's fastened." Another voice: "And this...." Other voices, with increasing desperation, verified that every airlock was implacably sealed fast by the presence of air pressure inside the lock itself.

Time was passing. Joe had never noticed, before, the minute noises of the air pressure apparatus strapped to his back. His exhaled breath went to a tiny pump that forced it through a hygroscopic filter which at once extracted excess moisture and removed carbon dioxide. The same pump carefully measured a volume of oxygen equal to the removed CO_2 and added it to the air it released. The pump made very small sounds indeed, and the valves were almost noiseless, but Joe could hear their clickings.

Something burned him. He had been standing perfectly still while trying to concentrate on a way out. Sunshine had shone uninterruptedly on one side of his space suit for as long as five minutes. Despite the insulation inside, that was too long. He turned quickly to expose another part of himself to the sunlight. He knew abstractedly that the metal underfoot would sear bare flesh that touched it. A few yards away, in the shadow, the metal of the hull would be cold enough to freeze hydrogen. But here it was fiercely hot. It would melt solder. It might--

Mike was fumbling tin cans out of the net bag from which Haney had been throwing them away. He was a singular small figure, standing on shining steel, looking at one tin can after another and impatiently putting them aside.

He found one that seemed to suit him. It was a large can. He knelt with it, pressing a part of it to the hot metal of the satellite's hull. A moment later he was ripping it apart. The solder had softened. He unrolled a sort of cylinder, then bent again, using the curved inner surface to concentrate the intolerable sunshine.

Joe caught his breath at the implication. Concentrated sunshine can be incredibly hot. Starting with unshielded, empty-space sunshine, practically any imaginable temperature is possible with a large enough mirror. Mike didn't have a concave mirror. He had only a cylindrical one. He couldn't reflect light to a point, but only to a line. Mike couldn't hope to do more than double or triple the temperature of a given spot. But considering what he wore on his back--!

Joe made his way clumsily to the spot where Mike now gesticulated to Haney, trying to convey his meaning by gestures since Sanford would overhear any spoken word.

"I get it, Mike," said Joe. "I'll help." He added: "Chief! You watch Sanford. The rest of you try to flatten out some tin cans or find some with flat round ends!"

He reached the spot where Mike bent over the plating. His hand moved to cast a shadow where the light had played.

"I need more reflectors," Mike said brusquely, "but we can do it!"

Joe beckoned. There were more, hurried clankings. Space-suited figures gathered about.

The Platform rolled on through space. Where it was bright it was very, very bright, and where it was dark it was blackness. Off in emptiness the many-colored mass of Earth shone hugely, rolling past. Innumerable incurious stars looked on. The sun flamed malevolently. The moon floated abstractedly far away.

Mike was bent above a small round airlock door. He had a distorted half-cylinder of sheet tin between his space-gloved hands. It reflected a line of intensified sunlight to the edge of the airlock seal. Haney ripped fiercely at other tin cans. Joe held another strip of polished metal. It focused crudely--very crudely--on top of Mike's line of reflected sunshine. Someone else held the end of a tin can to reflect more sunshine. Someone else had a larger disk of tin.

They stood carefully still. It looked completely foolish. There were six men in frozen attitudes, trying to reflect sunshine down to a single blindingly-bright spot on an airlock door. They seemed breathlessly tense. They ignored the glories of the firmament. They were utterly absorbed in trying to make a spot of unbearable brightness glow more brightly still.

Mike moved his hand to cast a shadow. The steel was a little more than red-hot for the space of an inch. It would not melt, of course. It could not. And they had no tools to bend or pierce the presumably softened metal. But Mike said fiercely:

"Keep it hot!"

He squirmed. His space suit was fabric, like the rest, but it had been cut down to permit him to use it. It was bulkier on him than the suits of the others. He shifted his shoulder pack. The brass valve-nipple by which the oxygen tank was filled....

He jammed a ragged fragment of tin in place. He pressed down fiercely. A blazing jet of fierce, scintillating, streaking sparks leaped up from the spot where the metal glowed brightly. A hollow in the metal plate appeared. The metal disintegrated in gushing flecks of light....

White-hot iron in pure oxygen happens to be inflammable. Iron is not incombustible at all. Powdered steel, ground fine enough, will burn if simply exposed to air. Really fine steel wool will make an excellent blaze if a match is touched to it. White-hot iron, with a jet of oxygen played upon it, explodes to steaming sparks. Technically, Mike had used the perfectly well-known trick of an oxygen lance to pierce the airlock door, let the air out of the lock, and so allow the outer door to be opened.

There was a rush of vapor. The door was drilled through. Haney picked Mike up bodily, Joe heaved the door open, and Haney climbed into it, practically carrying Mike by the scruff of the neck. Joe panted, "Plug the hole from the inside. Sit on it if you have to!" and slammed the door shut.

They waited. Sanford's voice came in the ear-phones. It was higher in pitch than it had been.

"You fools!" he raged. "It's useless! It's stupid to do useless things! It's stupid to do anything at all--"

There were sudden scuffling clankings. Joe swung about. The Chief and Sanford were struggling. Sanford flailed his arms about, trying to break the Chief's faceplate while he screamed furious things about futility.

The Chief got exactly the hold he wanted. He lifted Sanford from the metal deck. He could have thrown him away to emptiness, then, but he did not.

He set Sanford in mid-space as if upon a shelf. The raging man hung in the void an exact man-height above the Platform's surface. The Chief drew back and left him there, Sanford could writhe there for a century before the Platform's infinitesimal gravity brought him down.

"Huh!" said the Chief wrathfully. "How's Haney and Mike making out?"

Almost on the instant, twenty yards away, a tiny airlock door thrust out from the surface of glittering metal, and helmet and antenna appeared.

"You guys can come in now," said Haney's voice in Joe's headphones. "It's all okay. Mike's pumping out the other locks too, so you can come in at any of 'em."

The space-suited figures clumped loudly to airlock doors. There were a dozen or more small airlocks in various parts of the hull, besides the great door to admit supply ships. The Chief growled and moved toward Sanford now raging like the madman his helplessness made him.

"No," said Joe shortly. "He'd fight again. Go inside. That's an order, Chief."

The Chief grunted and obeyed. Joe went to the nearest airlock and entered the great steel hull.

Sanford floated in emptiness, two yards from the Space Platform he would have turned into a derelict. He did not move farther away. He did not fall toward it. There was nobody to listen to him. He cried out in blood-curdling fury because other men were smarter than he was. Other men had solved problems he could not solve. Other men were his superiors. He screamed his rage.

Presently the Platform revolved slowly beneath him. It was turned, of course, by the monster gyros which in turn were controlled by the pilot gyros Joe and Haney and the Chief and Mike had repaired when saboteurs smashed them.

The Platform rotated sedately. A great gap appeared in it. The door of the supply ship lock moved until Sanford, floating helplessly, was opposite its mouth.

A rod with a rounded object at its end appeared past the docked supply ship. It reached out and touched Sanford's helmet. It was the magnetic grapple which drew space ships into their dock.

It drew Sanford, squirming and streaming, into the great lock. The outer doors closed. Before air was admitted to the inside, Sanford went suddenly still.

When they took him out of his suit he was apparently unconscious. He could not be roused. Freed, he drew his knees up to his chin in the position in which primitive peoples bury their dead. He seemed to sleep. Brent examined him carefully.

"Catatonia," he said distastefully. "He spent his life thinking he was smarter than anybody else--smarter, probably, than all the universe. He believed it. He couldn't face the fact that he was wrong. He couldn't stay conscious and not know it. So he's blacked out. He refuses to be anything unless he can be smartest. We'll have to do artificial feeding and all that until we can get him down to Earth to a hospital." He shrugged.

"We'd better report this down to Earth," Joe said. "By the way, better not describe our screen of tin cans on radio waves. Not even microwaves. It might leak. And we want to see if it works."

Just forty-two hours later they found out that it did work. A single rocket came climbing furiously out from Earth. It came from the night-side, and they could not see where it was launched, though they could make excellent guesses. They got a single guided missile ready to crash it if necessary.

It wasn't necessary. The bomb from Earth detonated 300 miles below the artificial satellite. Its proximity fuse, sending out small radar-type waves, had them reflected back by an empty sardine can thrown away from the Platform by Mike Scandia forty-some hours ago. The sardine can had been traveling in its own private orbit ever since. The effect of Mike's muscles had not been to send it back to Earth, but to change the center of the circular orbit in which it floated. Sometimes it floated above the Platform--that was on one side of Earth--and sometimes below it. It was about 300 miles under the Platform when it reflected urgent, squealing radar frequency waves to a complex proximity fuse in the climbing rocket. The rocket couldn't tell the difference between a sardine can and a Space Platform.

It exploded with a blast of pure brightness like that of the sun.

The Platform went on its monotonous round about the planet from which it had risen only weeks before. Sanford was strapped in a bunk and fed through a tube, and on occasion massaged and variously tended to keep him alive. The men on the Platform worked. They made telephoto maps of Earth. They took highly magnified, long-exposure photographs of Mars, pictures that could not possibly be made with such distinctness from the bottom of Earth's turbulent ocean of air.

There was a great deal of official business to be done. Weather observations of the form and distribution of cloud masses were an important matter. The Platform could make much more precise measurements of the solar constant than could be obtained below. The flickering radar was gathering information for studies of the frequency and size of meteoric particles outside the atmosphere. There was the extremely important project for securing and sealing in really good vacua in various electronic devices brought up by Joe and his crew in the supply ship.

But sometimes Joe managed to talk to Sally.

It was very satisfying to see her on the television screen in personal conversation. Their talk couldn't be exactly private, because it could be picked up elsewhere. It probably was. But she told Joe how she felt, and she wanted to read him the newspaper stories based on the reports Brent had sent down. Brent was in command of the Platform now that Sanford lay in a resolute coma in his bunk. But Joe discouraged such waste of time.

"How's the food?" asked Sally. "Are you people getting any fresh vegetables from the hydroponic garden?"

They were, and Joe told her so. The huge chamber in which sun-lamps glowed for a measured number of hours in each twenty-four produced incredibly luxuriant vegetation. It kept the air of the ship breathable. It even changed the smell of it from time to time, so that there was no feeling of staleness.

"And the cooking system's really good?" she wanted to know. Sally was partly responsible for that, too. "And how about the bunks?"

"I sleep now," Joe admitted.

That had been difficult. It was possible to get used to weightlessness while awake. One would slip, sometimes, and find himself suddenly tense and panicky because he'd abruptly noticed all over again that he was falling. But--and yet again Sally was partly responsible--the bunks were designed to help in that difficulty. Each bunk had an inflatable top blanket. One crawled in and settled down, and turned the petcock that inflated the cover. Then it held one quite gently but reassuringly in place. It was possible to stir and to turn over, but the feeling of being held fast was very comforting. With a little care about what one thought of before going to sleep, one could get a refreshing eight hours' rest. The bunks were luxury.

Sally said: "The date and time's a secret, of course, because it might be overheard, but there'll be another ship up before too long. It's bringing landing rockets for you to come back with."

"That's good!" said Joe. It would feel good to set foot on solid ground again. He looked at Sally and said eagerly, "We've got a date the evening I get back?"

"We've got a date," she said, nodding.

But it couldn't very well be a definite date. There were people with ideas that ran counter to plans for Joe to get back to Earth and a date with Sally Holt. The Space Platform was not admired uniformly by all the nations of Earth. The United States had built it because the United Nations couldn't, and one of the attractions of the idea had been that once it got out to space and was armed, peace must reign upon Earth because it could smack down anybody who made war.

The trouble was that it wasn't armed well enough. Six guided missiles couldn't defend it indefinitely. It looked as helpless as isolated Berlin did before the first airlift proved what men and planes could do in the way of transport. And the Platform's enemies didn't intend for it to be saved by a rocketlift. They would try to smash it before such a lift could get started.

A week after Joe got to it with the guided missiles, three rockets attacked. They went up from somewhere in the middle of the Pacific. One blew up 250 miles below the Platform. Another detonated 190 miles away. For safety's sake the third was crashed--at the cost of one guided missile--when it had come within 50 miles.

The screen of tin cans worked, but it wasn't thick enough. The occupants of the Platform went about hunting for sheet metal that could be spared. They pulled out minor partitions here and there, and went out on the surface and threw away thousands of small glittering scraps of metal in all directions.

Two weeks later, there was another attack. It could be calculated that Joe couldn't have carried up more than six guided missiles. There might be as few as two of them left. So eight rockets came up together--and the first of them went off 400 miles from the Platform. Only one got as close as 200 miles. No guided missiles were expended in defense.

The Platform's enemies tried once more. This time the rockets arched up above the Platform's orbit and dived on the satellite from above. There were two of them. They went off at 180 and 270 miles from the Platform. Joe's trash screen would not work on Earth, but in space it was an adequate defense against anything equipped with proximity fuses. It could be assumed that in a full-scale space-war nuts, bolts, rusty nails and beer bottle caps would become essential military equipment.

Three days after this last attack, a second supply ship took off from Earth. Lieutenant Commander Brown was a passenger. Its start was just like the one Joe's ship had made. Pushpots lifted it, jatos hurled it on, and then the furious, flaming take-off rockets drove it valiantly out toward the stars.

Joe's ship had been moved out of the landing lock and was moored against the Platform's hull. The second ship made contact in two hours and seventeen minutes from take-off. It arrived with its own landing rockets intact, and it brought a set of forty-foot metal tubes for Joe's ship to get back to Earth with. But those landing rockets and Lieutenant Commander Brown constituted all its payload. It couldn't bring up anything else.

And Lieutenant Commander Brown called a very formal meeting in the huge living space at the Platform's center. He stood up grandly in full uniform--and had to hook his feet around a chair leg to keep from floating absurdly in mid-air. This detracted slightly from the dignity of his stance, but not from the official voice with which he read two documents aloud.

The first paper detached Lieutenant Commander Brown from his regular naval duties and assigned him pro tem to service with the Space Exploration Project. The second was an order directing him to take command and assume direction of the Space Platform.

Having read his orders, he cleared his throat and said cordially, "I am honored to serve here with you. Frankly, I expect to learn much from you and to have very few orders to give. I expect merely to exercise such authority as experience at sea has taught me is necessary for a tight and happy ship. I trust this will be one."

He beamed. Nobody was impressed. It was perfectly obvious that he'd simply been sent up to acquire experience in space for later naval use, and that he'd been placed in command because it was unthinkable that he serve under anyone without official rank and authority. And he quite honestly believed that his coming, with experience in command, was a blessing to the Platform. In fact, there was no danger that this commander of the Platform would crack up under stress as Sanford had.

But it was too bad that he hadn't brought some long-range guided missiles with him.

Joe's ship had brought up twenty tons of cargo and twenty tons of landing rockets. The second ship brought up twenty tons of landing rockets for Joe, and twenty tons of landing rockets for itself. That was all. The second trip out to the Space Platform was a rescue mission and nothing else. Arithmetic wouldn't let it be anything else. And there couldn't be any idea of noble self-sacrifice and staying out at the Platform, either, because only four ships like Joe's had been begun, and only two were even near completion. Joe's had taken off the instant it was finished. The second had done the same. The second pair of spaceships wouldn't be ready for two months or more. The ships that could be used had to be used.

So, only thirty-six hours after the arrival of the second rocketship at the Platform, the two of them took off together to return to Earth. Joe's ship left the airlock first. Sanford was loaded in the cabin of the other ship as cargo. Lieutenant Commander Brown stayed out at the Platform to replace him.

Obviously, in order to get back to Earth they headed away from it in fleet formation. They pointed their rounded noses toward the Milky Way.

The upward course was an application of the principle that made the screen of tin cans and oddments remain about the Platform. Each of those small objects had had the Platform's own velocity and orbit. Thrown away from it, the centers of their orbits changed. In theory, the center of the Platform's orbit was the center of Earth. But the centers of the orbits of the thrown-away objects were pushed a few miles--twenty--fifty--a hundred--away from the center of Earth.

The returning space ships also had the orbit and speed of the Platform. They wanted to shift the centers of their orbits by very nearly 4,000 miles, so that at one point they would just barely graze Earth's atmosphere, lose some speed to it, and then bounce out to empty space again before they melted. Cooled off, they'd make another grazing bounce. After eight such bounces they'd stay in the air, and the stubby fins would give them a sort of gliding angle and controllability, while the landing rockets would let them down to solid ground. Or so it was hoped.

Meanwhile they headed out instead of in toward Earth. They went out on their steering-rockets only, using the liquid fuel that had not been needed for course correction on the way out. At 4,000 miles up, the force of gravity is just one-fourth of that at the Earth's surface. It still exists; it is merely canceled out in an orbit. The ships could move outward at less cost in fuel than they could move in.

So they went out and out on parallel courses, and the Platform dwindled behind them. Night flowed below until the hull of the artificial satellite shone brightly against a background of seeming sheer nothingness.

The twilight zone of Earth's shadow reached the Platform. It glowed redly, glowed crimson, glowed the deepest possible color that could be seen, and winked out. The ships climbed on, using their tiny steering rockets.

Nothing happened. The ships drew away from each other for safety. They were 50, then 60 miles apart. One glowed red and vanished in the shadow of the Earth. The other was extinguished in the same way. Then they went hurtling through the blackness of the night side of Earth. Microwaves from the ground played upon them--radar used by friend and foe alike--and the friendly radar guided tight-beam communicator waves to them with comforting assurance that their joint course and height and speed were exactly the calculated optimum. But they could not be seen at all.

When they appeared again they were still farther out from Earth than the Platform's orbit, but no farther from each other. And they were descending. The centers of their orbits had been displaced very, very far indeed.

Going out, naturally, the ships had lost angular speed as they gained in height. Descending, they gained in angular velocity as they lost height. They were not quite 30 miles apart as they sped with increasing, headlong speed and rushed toward the edge of the world's disk. When they were only 2,000 miles high, the Earth's surface under them moved much faster than it had on the way up. When they were only 1,000 miles high, the seas and continents seemed to flow past like a rushing river. At 500 miles, mountains and plains were just distinguishable as they raced past underneath. At 200 miles there was merely a churning, hurtling surface on which one could not focus one's eyes because of the speed of its movement.

They missed the solid surface of Earth by barely 40 miles. They were moving at a completely impossible speed. The energy of their position 4,000 miles high had been transformed into kinetic energy of motion. And at 40 miles there is something very close to a vacuum, compared to sea-level. But compared to true emptiness, and at the speed of meteors, the thin air had a violent effect.

A thin humming sound began. It grew louder. The substance of the ship was responding to the impact of the thin air upon it. The sound rose to a roar, to a bellow, to a thunderous tumult. The ship quivered and trembled. It shook. A violent vibration set up and grew more and more savage. The whole ship shook with a dreadful persistence, each vibration more monstrous, more straining, more ominous than before.

The four in the space ship cabin knew torture. Weight returned to them, weight more violent than the six gravities they had known for a bare fourteen seconds at take-off. But that, at least, had been smoothly applied. This was deceleration at a higher figure yet, and accompanied by the shaking of bodies which weighed seven times as much as ever before--and bodies, too, which for weeks past had been subject to no weight at all.

They endured. Nothing at all could be done. At so many miles per second no possible human action could be determined upon and attempted in time to have any effect upon the course of the ship. Joe could see out a quartzite port. The ground 40 miles below was merely a blur. There was a black sky overhead, which did not seem to stir. But cloud-masses rushed at express-train speed below him, and his body weighed more than half a ton, and the ship made the sound of innumerable thunders and shook, and shook and shook....

And then, when it seemed that it must fly utterly to pieces, the thunder diminished gradually to a bellow, and the bellow to a roar, and the roaring.... And the unthinkable weight oppressing him grew less.

The Earth was farther away and moving farther still. They were 100 miles high. They were 200 miles high....

There was no longer any sound at all, except their gaspings for breath. Their muscles had refused to lift their chests at all during the most brutal of the deceleration period.

Presently Joe croaked a question. He looked at the hull-temperature indicators. They were very, very high. He found that he was bruised where he had strapped himself in. The places where each strap had held his heavy body against the ship's vibrations were deeply black-and-blue.

The Chief said thickly: "Joe, somehow I don't think this is going to work. When do we hit again?"

"Three hours plus or minus something," said Joe, dry-throated. "We'll hear from the ground."

Mike said in a cracked voice: "Radar reports we went a little bit too low. They think we weren't tilted up far enough. We didn't bounce as soon as we should."

Joe unstrapped himself.

"How about the other ship?"

"It did better than we did," said Mike. "It's a good 200 miles ahead. Down at the Shed, they're recalculating for us. We'll have to land with six grazes instead of eight. We lost too much speed."

Joe went staggering, again weightless, to look out a port for the other ship. He should have known better. One does not spot an eighty-foot space ship with the naked eye when it is 200 miles away.

But he saw something, though for seconds he didn't know what it was.

Now the little ship was 300 miles high and still rising. Joe was dazed and battered by the vibration of the ship in the graze just past. The sister space ship hadn't lost speed so fast. It would be traveling faster. It would be leaving him farther behind every second. It was rising more sharply. It would rise higher.

Joe stared numbly out of a port, thinking confusedly that his hull would be dull red on its outer surface, though the heating had been so fast that the inner surfaces of the plating might still be cold. He saw the vast area which was the curve of the edge of the world. He saw the sunlight upon clouds below and glimpses of the surface of the Earth itself.

And he saw something rising out of the mists at the far horizon. It was a thread of white vapor. The other rocketship was a speck, a mote, invisible because of its size and distance. This thread of vapor was already 100 miles long, and it expanded to a column of whiteness half a mile across before it seemed to dissipate. It rose and rose, as if following something which sped upward. It was a rocket trail. The violence of its writhings proved the fury with which the rocket climbed.

It was on its way to meet the other space ship.

It did. Joe saw the thread of vapor extend and grow until it was higher than he was. He never saw the other ship, which was too small. But he saw the burst of flame, bright as the sun itself, which was the explosion of a proximity fuse bomb. He knew, then, that nothing but incandescent, radioactive gas remained of the other ship and its crew.

Then he saw the trail of the second rocket. It was rising to meet him.

5

The four of them watched through the ports as the thread of vapor sped upward. They hated the rocket and the people who had built it. Joe said between his teeth, "We could spend our landing-rockets and make it chase us, but it'll have fuel for that!"

The Chief muttered in Mohawk. The words sounded as if they ought to have blue fire at their edges and smell of sulphur. Mike the midget said crackling things in his small voice. Haney stared, his eyes burning.

Their ship was a little over 400 miles up, now. The rocket was 100 or better. The rendezvous would be probably 200 miles ahead and correspondingly higher. The rocket was accelerating furiously. It had farther to travel, but its rate of climb was already enormous and it increased every second.

The ship could swing to right or left on steering rockets, but the war rocket could swerve also. It was controlled from the ground. It did not need to crash the small ship from space. Within a limited number of miles the blast of its atomic warhead would vaporize any substance that could exist. And of course the ship could not turn back. Even the expenditure of all its landing-rockets could not bring twenty tons of ship to a halt. They could speed it up, so it would pass the calculated meeting place ahead of the war rocket. But the bomb would simply follow in a stern chase. In any case, the ship could not stop.

But neither could the rocket.

Joe never knew how he saw the significance of that fact. On land or sea, of course, an automobile or a ship moves in the direction in which it is pointed. Even an airplane needs to make only minor corrections for air currents which affect it. But an object in space moves on a course which is the sum of all its previous speeds and courses. Joe's ship was moving eastward above the Earth at so many miles per second. If he drove north--at a right angle to his present course--the ship would not cease to move to the east. It would simply move northward in addition to moving east. If the rocket from Earth turned north or east it would continue to move up and merely add the other motion to its vertical rise.

Joe stared at the uncoiling thread of vapor which was the murder rocket's trail. He hated it so fiercely that he wanted to escape it even at the cost of destruction, merely to foil its makers. At one moment, he was hardly aware of anything but his own fury and the frantic desire to frustrate the rocket at any cost. The next instant, somehow, he was not angry at all. Because somehow his brain had dredged up the fact that the war rocket could no more turn back than he could--and he saw its meaning.

"Mike!" he snapped sharply. "Get set! Report what we do! Everybody set for acceleration! Steering rockets ready, Chief! Get set to help, Haney! I don't know whether we'll get out of this alive, but we'd better get into our space suits."

Then he literally dived back to his acceleration chair and strapped in in feverish haste. The ship was then a quarter of the way to the meeting place and the rocket had very much farther to go. But it was rising faster.

The ship's gyros whined and squealed as Joe jammed on their controls. The little ship spun in emptiness. Its bow turned and pointed down. The steering rockets made their roarings.

Joe found himself panting. "The--rocket's rising faster--than we are. It's been gaining--altitude maybe--two minutes. It's lighter than when--it started but--it can't stop--less than a minute, anyhow so we duck under it----"

He did not make computations. There was no time. The war rocket might have started at four or five gravities acceleration, but it would speed up as its fuel burned. It might be accelerating at fifteen gravities now, and have an attained velocity of four miles a second and still increasing. If the little ship ducked under it, it could not kill that rate-of-climb in time to follow in a stern chase.

"Haney!" panted Joe. "Watch out the port! Are we going to make it?"

Haney crawled forward. Joe had forgotten the radar because he'd seen the rocket with his own eyes. It seemed to need eyes to watch it. Mike spoke curtly into the microphone broadcasting to ground. He was reporting each action and order as it took place and was given. There was no time to explain anything. But Mike thought of the radar. He watched it.

It showed the vast curve of Earth's surface, 400 miles down. It showed a moving pip, much too much nearer, which was the war rocket. Mike made a dot on the screen with a grease pencil where the pip showed. It moved. He made another dot. The pip continued to move. He made other dots.

They formed a curving line--curved because the rocket was accelerating--which moved inexorably toward the center of the radar screen. The curve would cut the screen's exact center. That meant collision.

"Too close, Joe!" said Mike shrilly. "We may miss it, but not enough!"

"Then hold fast," yelled Joe. "Landing rockets firing, three--two--one!"

The bellowing of the landing-rockets smote their ears. Weight seized upon them, three gravities of acceleration toward the rushing flood of clouds and solidity which was the Earth. The ship plunged downward with all its power. It was intolerable--and ten times worse because they had been weightless so long and were still shaken and sore and bruised from the air-graze only minutes back.

Mike took acceleration better than the others, but his voice was thin when he gasped, "Looks--like this does it, Joe!" Seconds later he gasped again, "Right! The rocket's above us and still going away!"

The gyros squealed again. The ship plunged into vapor which was the trail of the enemy rocket. For an instant the flowing confusion which was Earth was blotted out. Then it was visible again. The ship was plunging downward, but its sidewise speed was undiminished and much greater than its rate of fall.

"Mike," panted Joe. "Get the news out. What we did--and why. I'm--going to turn the ship's head back on our--course. We can't slow enough but--I'd rather crash on Earth than let them blast us----"

The ship turned again. It pointed back in the direction from which it had come. With the brutal sternward pressure produced by the landing-rockets, it felt as if it were speeding madly back where it had come from. It was the sensation they'd felt when the ship took off from Earth, so long before. But then the cloud masses and the earth beneath had flowed toward the ship and under it. Now they flowed away. The appearance was that of an unthinkably swift wake left behind by a ship at sea. The Earth's surface fled away and fled away from them.

"Crazy, this!" Joe muttered thickly. "If the ship were lighter--or we had more power--we could land! I'm sorry, but I'd rather----"

Haney turned his head from where he clung near the bow-ports. His features changed slowly as he talked because of acceleration-driven blood engorging his lips and bloating his cheeks. After one instant he closed his eyes fiercely. They felt as if they would pop out of his head. He gasped, "Yes! Get down to air-resistance. A chance--not good but a chance--ejection seats--with space suits--might make it...."

He began to let himself back toward his acceleration chair. He could not possibly have climbed forward. It was a horrible task to let himself down, with triple his normal weight pulling at him and after the beating taken a little while ago.

Sweat stood out on his skin as he lowered himself sternward. Once his grip on a hand-line slipped and he had to sustain the drag of nearly six hundred pounds by a single hand and arm. It would not be a good idea to fall at three gravities.

The landing rockets roared and roared, and Joe tilted the bow down a little farther, so that the streaming flood of clouds drew nearer.

Haney got to his acceleration chair. He let himself into it and his eyes closed.

Mike's sharp voice barked: "What's the chance, Haney?"

Haney's mouth opened, and closed, and opened again. "Rocket flames," he gasped, "pushed back--wind--splash on hull--may melt--lighten weight--hundred to one against----"

The odds were worse than that. The ship couldn't land because its momentum was too great for the landing rockets to cancel out. If it had weighed five tons instead of twenty, landing might have been possible. Haney was saying that if the ship were to be lowered into air while rushing irresistibly sternward despite its rockets, that the rocket flames might be splashed out by the wind. Instead of streaking astern in a lance-like shape, they might be pushed out like a rocket blast when it hits the earth in a guided missile take-off. Such a blast spreads out flat in all directions. Here the rocket flames might be spread by wind until they played upon the hull of the ship. If they did, they might melt it as they melted their own steel cases in firing. And three-fourths or more of the hull might be torn loose from the cabin bow section. So much was unlikely, but it was possible.

The impossible odds were that the four could survive even if the cabin were detached. They were decelerating at three gravities now. If part of the ship burned or melted or was torn away, the rocket thrust might speed the cabin up to almost any figure. And there is a limit to the number of gravities a man can take, even in an acceleration chair.

Nevertheless, that was what Haney proposed. They were due to be killed anyhow. Joe tried it.

He dived into atmosphere. At 60 miles altitude a thin wailing seemed to develop without reason. At 40 miles, the ship had lost more than two miles per second of its speed since the landing-rockets were ignited, and there was a shuddering in all its fabric--though because of the loss of speed it was not as bad as the atmosphere-graze. At 30 it began to shake and tremble. At 25 miles high there was as horrible a vibration and as deadly a deceleration as at the air-graze. At 12 miles above the surface of the Earth the hull temperature indicators showed the hind part of the hull at red heat. The ship happened to be traveling backward at several times the speed of sound, and air could not move away from before it. It was compressed to white heat at the entering surface, and the metal plating went to bright red heat at that point. But the hull just aft of the rocket mouths was hotter still. There the splashing rocket flames bathed it in intolerable incandescence. Hull plates, braces and beams glared white----

The tip of the tail caved in. The ship's empty cargo space was instantly filled with air at intolerable pressure and heat.

The hull exploded outward where the rocket flames played. There was a monstrous, incredible jerking of the cabin that remained. That fraction of the ship received the full force of the rocket thrust. They could decelerate it at a rate of fifteen gravities or more.

They did.

Joe lost consciousness as instantly and as peacefully as if he had been hit on the jaw.

An unknown but brief time later, he found himself listening with a peculiar astonishment. The rockets had burned out. They had lasted only seconds after the separation of the ship into two fragments. Radars on the ground are authority for this. Those few seconds were extremely important. The cabin lost an additional half-mile per second of velocity, which was enough to make the difference between the cabin heating up too, and the cabin being not quite destroyed.

The cabin remnant was heavy, of course, but it was an irregular object, some twenty feet across. It was below orbital velocity, and wind-resistance slowed it. Even so, it traveled 47 miles to the east in falling the last 10 miles to Earth. It hit a hillside and dug itself a 70-foot crater in the ground.

But there was nobody in it, then. A little over a month before, it had seemed to Joe that ejection seats were the most useless of all possible pieces of equipment to have in a space ship. He'd been as much mistaken as anybody could be. With an ejection seat, a jet pilot can be shot out of a plane traveling over Mach one, and live to tell about it. This crumpling cabin fell fast, but Joe stuffed Mike in an ejection seat and shot him out. He and the Chief dragged Haney to a seat, and then the Chief shoved Joe off--and the four of them, one by one, were flung out into a screaming stream of air. But the ribbon-parachutes did not burst. They nearly broke the necks of their passengers, but they let them down almost gently.

And it was quite preposterous, but all four landed intact. Mike, being lightest and first to be ejected, came down by himself in a fury because he'd been treated with special favor. The Chief and Joe landed almost together. After a long time, Joe staggered out of his space suit and harness and tried to help the Chief, and they held each other up as they stumbled off together in search of Haney.

When they found him he was sleeping heavily, exhausted, in a canebrake. He hadn't even bothered to disengage his parachute harness or take off his suit.

6

A good deal of that landing remained confused in Joe's mind. While it was going on he was much too busy to be absorbing impressions. When he landed, he was as completely exhausted as anybody wants to be. It was only during the next day that he even tried to sort out his recollections.

Then he woke up suddenly, with a muffled roaring going on all about him. He blinked his eyes open and listened. Presently he realized what the noise was, and wondered that he hadn't realized before. It was the roaring of the motors of a multi-engined plane. He knew, without remembering the details at the moment, that he and the other three were on a plane bound across the Pacific for America. He was in a bunk--and he felt extraordinarily heavy. He tried to move, and it was an enormous effort to move his arm. He struggled to turn over, and found straps holding his body down.

He fumbled at them. They had readily releasable clasps, and he loosened them easily. After a bit he struggled to sit upright. He was horribly heavy or horribly weak. He couldn't tell which. And each separate muscle in his whole body ached. Twinges of pain accompanied every movement. He sat up, swaying a little with the slow movements of the plane, and gradually, things came back.

The landing in the ribbon-chute. They'd come down somewhere on the west coast of India, not too far from the sea. He remembered crashing into the edge of a thin jungle and finding the Chief, and the two of them searching out Haney and stumbling to open ground. After laying out a signal for air searchers, they went off into worn-out slumber while they waited.

He remembered that there'd been a patrol of American destroyers in the Arabian Sea, as everywhere under the orbit of the Platform. Their radar had reported the destruction of one space ship and the frantic diving of the other, its division into two parts, and then the tiny objects, which flew out from the smaller cabin section, which had descended as only ejection-seat parachutes could possibly have done. Two destroyers steamed onward underneath those drifting specks, to pick them up when they should come down. But the other nearby destroyers had other business in hand.

The two trailing destroyers reached Goa harbor within hours of the landing of the four from space. A helicopter found the first three of them within hours after that. They were twenty miles inland and thirty south from Goa. Mike wasn't located until the next day. He'd been shot out of the ship's cabin earlier and higher; he was lighter, and he'd floated farther.

But things--satisfying things--had happened in the interval. Sitting almost dizzily on the bunk in the swiftly roaring plane while blood began sluggishly to flow through his body, Joe remembered the gleeful, unofficial news passed around on the destroyers. They waited for Mike to be brought in. But they rejoiced vengefully.

The report was quite true, but it never reached the newspapers. Nobody would ever admit it, but the rockets aimed at the returning space ships had been spotted by Navy radar as they went up from the Arabian Sea. And the ships of the radar patrol couldn't do anything about the rockets, but they could and did converge savagely upon the places from which they had been launched. Planes sped out to spot and bomb. Destroyers arrived.

Somewhere there was a navy department that could write off two modern submarines with rocket-launching equipment, last heard from west of India. American naval men would profess bland ignorance of any such event, but there were acres of dead fish floating on the ocean where depth-bombs had hunted down and killed two shapes much too big to be fish, which didn't float when they were killed and which would never report back how they'd destroyed two space ships. There'd be seagulls feasting over that area, and there'd be vague tales about the happening in the bazaars of Hadhramaut. But nobody would ever admit knowing anything for certain.

But Joe knew. He got to his feet, wobbling a little bit in the soaring plane. He ached everywhere. His muscles protested the strain of holding him erect. He held fast, summoning strength. Before his little ship broke up he'd been shaken intolerably, and his body had weighed half a ton. Where his safety-belt had held him, his body was one wide bruise. There'd been that killing acceleration when the ship split in two. The others--except Mike--were in as bad a case or worse. Haney and the Chief were like men who'd been rolled down Mount Everest in a barrel. All of them had slept for fourteen hours straight before they even woke up for food. Even now, Joe didn't remember boarding this plane or getting into the bunk. He'd probably been carried in.

Joe stood up, doggedly, until enough strength came to him to justify his sitting down again. He began to dress. It was astonishing how many places about his body were sore to the touch. It was startling how heavy his arms and legs felt, and how much of an effort even sitting erect was. But he began to remember Mike's adventure, and managed to grin feebly. It was the only thing worth a smile in all the things that had happened.

Because Mike's landing had been quite unlike the others. Joe and the Chief landed near the edge of a jungle. Haney landed in a canebrake. But Mike came floating down from the sky, swaying splendidly, into the estate of a minor godling.

He was relatively unharmed by the shaking-up he'd had. The strength of muscles depends on their cross-section, but their weight depends on their volume. The strength of a man depends on the square of his size, but his weight on the cube. So Mike had taken the deceleration and the murderous vibration almost in his stride. He floated longer and landed more gently than the rest.

Joe grinned painfully at the memory of Mike's tale. He'd come on board the rescue destroyer in a towering, explosive rage. When his ribbon-parachute let him down out of the sky, it deposited him gently on ploughed fields not far from a small and primitive Hindu village. He'd been seen to descend from the heavens. He was a midget--not as other men--and he was dressed in a space suit with glittering metal harness.

The pagan villagers greeted him with rapture.

When the searching-party found Mike, they were just in time to prevent a massacre--by Mike. Adoring natives had seized upon him, conveyed him in high state to a red mud temple, seemingly tried to suffocate him with evidences of their pride and joy at his arrival, and dark-skinned maidens were trying hopefully to win his approval of their dancing. But the rescue-party found him with a club in his hand and blood in his eye, setting out furiously to change the tone of his reception.

Joe still didn't know all the details, but he tried to concentrate on what he did know as he put his uniform on again. He didn't want to think how little it meant, now. The silver space ship badge didn't mean a thing, any more. There weren't any more space ships. The Platform wasn't a ship, but a satellite. There'd never been but two ships. Both had ceased to exist.

Joe walked painfully forward in the huge, roaring plane. The motors made a constant, humming thunder in his ears. It was not easy to walk. He held on to hand-holds as he moved. But he progressed past the bunk space. And there was Mike, sitting at a table and stuffing himself with good honest food. There was a glass port beside him, and Joe caught a glimpse of illimitable distances filled with cloud and sky and sea.

Mike nodded. He didn't offer to help Joe walk. That wouldn't have been practical. He waited until Joe sank into a seat opposite.

"Good sleep?" asked Mike.

"I guess so," said Joe. He added ruefully, "It hurts to nod, and I think it would hurt worse to shake my head. What's the matter with me, Mike? I didn't get banged up in the landing!"

"You got banged up before you landed," said Mike. "Worse than that, you spent better than six weeks out of gravity, where in an average day you took less actual exercise than a guy in bed with two broken legs!"

Joe eased himself back into his chair. He felt about 600 years old. Somebody poked a head into view and withdrew it. Joe lifted his arm and regarded it.

"Weighty! I guess you're right, Mike."

"I know I'm right!" said Mike. "If you spent six weeks in bed you'd expect to feel wobbly when you tried to walk. Up on the Platform you didn't even use energy to stand up! We didn't realize it, but we were living like invalids! We'll get our strength back, but next time we'll take measures. Huh! Take a trip to Mars in free fall, and by the time a guy got there his muscles'd be so flabby he couldn't stand up in half-gravity! Something's got to be done about that, Joe!"

Joe said sombrely, "Something's got to be done about space ships before that comes up again!"

Somebody appeared with a tray. There was food on it. Smoking hot food. Joe looked at it and knew that his appetite, anyhow, was back to Earth normal.

"Thanks!" he mumbled appreciatively, and attacked the food.

Mike drank his coffee. Then he said, "Joe, do you know anything about powder metallurgy?"

Joe shrugged. It hurt. "Powder metallurgy? Yes, I've seen it used, at my father's plant. They've made small precision parts with it. Why?"

"D'you know if anybody ever made a weld with it?" asked Mike.

Joe chewed. Then he said:

"I think so. Yes. At the plant they did. They had trouble getting the surfaces properly cleaned for welding. But they managed it. Why?"

"One more question," said Mike tensely. "How much Portland cement is used to make a cubic yard of concrete?"

"I wouldn't know," admitted Joe. "Why? What's all this about?"

"Haney and the Chief. Those two big apes have been kidding me--as long as they could stay awake--for what happened to me when I landed. Those infernal savages--" Mike seethed. "They got my clothes off and they had me smeared all over with butter and forty-'leven necklaces around my neck and flowers in my hair! They thought I was some kind of heathen god! Hanuman, somebody told me. The Hindu monkey-god!" He raged. "And those two big apes think it's funny! Joe, I never knew I *knew* all the words for the cussings I gave those heathen before our fellas found me! And Haney and the Chief will drive me crazy if I can't slap 'em down! Powder metallurgy does the trick, from what you told me. That's okay, then."

He stood up and stalked toward the front of the plane. Joe roused himself with an effort. He turned to look about him. Haney lay slumped in a reclining chair, on the other side of the plane cabin. His eyes were closed. The Chief lay limply in another chair. He smiled faintly at Joe, but he didn't try to talk. He was too tired. The return to normal gravity bothered him, as it did Joe.

Joe looked out the window. In neat, geometric spacing on either side of the transport there were fighter jets. There was another flight above and farther away. Joe saw, suddenly, a peeling-off of planes from the farther formation. They dived down through the clouds. He never knew what they went to look for or what they found. He went groggily back to his bunk in a strange and embarrassing weakness.

He woke when the plane landed. He didn't know where it might be. It was, he knew, an island. He could see the wide, sun-baked white of the runways. He could see sea-birds in clouds over at the edge. The plane trundled and lurched slowly to a stop. A service-truck came growling up, and somebody led cables from it up into the engines. Somebody watched dials, and waved a hand.

There was silence. There was stillness. Joe heard voices and footsteps. Presently he heard the dull booming of surf.

The plane seemed to wait for a very long time. Then there was a faint, faint distant whine of jets, and a plane came from the east. It was first a dot and then a vague shape, and then an infinitely graceful dark object which swooped down and landed at the other end of the strip. It came taxiing up alongside the transport ship and stopped.

An officer in uniform climbed out, waved his hand, and walked over to the transport. He climbed up the ladder and the pilot and co-pilot followed him. They took their places. The door closed. One by one, the jets chugged, then roared to life.

The officer talked to the pilot and co-pilot for a moment. He came down the aisle toward Joe. Mike the midget regarded him suspiciously.

The plane stirred. The newly arrived officer said pleasantly, "The Navy Department's sent me out here, Kenmore, to be briefed on what you know and to do a little briefing in turn."

The transport plane turned clumsily and began to taxi down the runway. It jolted and bumped over the tarmac, then lifted, and Joe saw that the island was nearly all airfield. There were a few small buildings and distance-dwarfed hangars. Beyond the field proper there was a ring of white surf. That was all. The rest was ocean.

"I haven't much briefing to do," admitted Joe.

Then he looked at the briefcase the other man opened. It had sheets and sheets of paper in it--hundreds, it seemed. They were filled with questions. He'd be called on to find answers for most of them, and to admit he didn't know the answers to the rest. When he was through with this questioning, every possible useful fact he knew would be on file for future use. And now he wrily recognized that this was part payment for the efficiency and speed with which the Navy had trailed them on their landing, and for the use of a transport plane to take them back to the United States.

"I'll try to answer what I can," he said cautiously. "But what're you to brief me about?"

"That you're not back on Earth yet," said the officer curtly, pulling out the first sheaf of questions. "Officially you haven't even started back. Ostensibly you're still on the Platform."

Joe blinked at him.

"If your return were known," continued the lieutenant, "the public would want to make heroes of you. First space travelers, and so on. They'd want you on television--all of you--telling about your adventures and your return. Inevitably, what happened to your ship would leak out. And if the public knew you'd been waylaid and shot down there'd be demands that the government take violent action to avenge the attack. It'd be something like the tumult over the sinking of the *Maine*, or the *Lusitania*--or even Pearl Harbor. It's much better for your return to be a secret for now."

Joe said wrily: "I don't think any of us want to be ridden around to have ticker-tape dumped on us. That part's all right. I'm sure the others will agree."

"Good! One more difficulty. We had two space ships. Now we have none. Our most likely enemies haven't only been building rockets, they've got a space fleet coming along. Intelligence just found out they're nearly ready for trial trips. They've been yelling to high heaven that we were building a space fleet to conquer the world. We weren't. They were. And it looks very much as if they may have beaten us."

The lieutenant got out the dreary mass of papers, intended to call for every conscious or unconscious observation Joe might have made in space. It was the equivalent of the interviews extracted from fliers after a bombing raid, and it was necessary, but Joe was very tired.

Wearily, he said, "Start your questions. I'll try to answer them."

They arrived in Bootstrap some forty-six hours after the crashing of their ship. Joe, at least, had slept nearly thirty of those hours. So while he was still wobbly on his feet and would be for days to come, his disposition was vastly improved.

There was nobody waiting on the airfield by the town of Bootstrap, but as they landed a black car came smoothly out and stopped close by the transport. Joe got down and climbed into it. Sally Holt was inside. She took both his hands and cried, and he was horribly embarrassed when the Chief came blundering into the car after him. But the Chief growled, "If he didn't kiss you, Sally, I'm going to kick his pants for him."

"He--he did," said Sally, gulping. "And I'm glad you're back, Chief. And Haney. And Mike."

Mike grinned as he climbed in the back too. Haney crowded in after him. They filled the rear of the car entirely. It started off swiftly across the field, swerving to the roadway that led to the highway out of Bootstrap to the Shed. It sped out that long white concrete ribbon, and the desert was abruptly all around them. Far ahead, the great round half-dome of the Shed looked like a cherry-pit on the horizon.

"It's good to be back!" said the Chief warmly. "I feel like I weigh a ton, but it's good to be back! Mike's the only one who was happier out yonder. He figures he belongs there. I got a story to tell you, Sally----"

"Chief!" said Mike fiercely. "Shut up!"

"Won't," said the Chief amiably. "Sally, this guy Mike----"

Mike went pale. "You're too big to kill," he said bitterly, "but I'll try it!"

The Chief grunted at him. "Quit being modest. Sally----"

Mike flung himself at the Chief, literally snarling. His small fist hit the Chief's face--and Mike was small but he was not puny. The "crack" of the impact was loud in the car. Haney grabbed. There was a moment's frenzied struggling. Then Mike was helplessly wrapped in Haney's arms, incoherent with fury and shame.

"Crazy fool!" grunted the Chief, feeling his jaw. "What's the matter with you? Don't you feel good?"

He was angry, but he was more concerned. Mike was white and raging.

"You tell that," he panted shrilly, "and so help me----"

"What's got into you?" demanded Haney anxiously. "I'd be bragging, I would, if I'd got a brainstorm like you did! That guy Sanford woulda wiped us all out----"

The Chief said angrily, between unease and puzzlement:

"I never knew you to go off your nut like this before! What's got into you, anyway?"

Mike gulped suddenly. Haney still held him firmly, but both Haney and the Chief were looking at him with worried eyes. And Mike said desperately: "You were going to tell Sally----"

The Chief snorted.

"Huh! You fool little runt! No! I was going to tell her about you opening up that airlock when Sanford locked us out! Sure I kidded you about what you're talking about! Sure! I'm going to do it again! But that's amongst us! I don't tell that outside!"

Haney made an inarticulate exclamation. He understood, and he was relieved. But he looked disgusted. He released Mike abruptly, rumbling to himself. He stared out the window. And Mike stood upright, an absurd small figure. His face worked a little.

"Okay," said Mike, with a little difficulty. "I was dumb. Only, Chief, you owe me a sock on the jaw when you feel like it. I'll take it."

He swallowed. Sally was watching wide-eyed.

"Sally," said Mike bitterly, "I'm a bigger fool than I look. I thought the Chief was going to tell you what happened when I landed. I--I floated down in a village over there in India, and those crazy savages'd never seen a parachute, and they began to yell and make gestures, and first thing I knew they had a sort of litter and were piling me in it, and throwing flowers all over me, and there was a procession----"

Sally listened blankly. Mike told the tale of his shame with the very quintessence of bitter resentment. When he got to his installation in a red-painted mud temple, and the reverent and forcible removal of his clothes so he could be greased with butter, Sally's lips began to twitch. At the picture of Mike in a red loincloth, squirming furiously while brown-skinned admirers zestfully sang his praises, howling his rage while they celebrated some sort of pious festival in honor of his arrival, Sally broke down and laughed helplessly.

Mike stared at her, aghast. He felt that he'd hated the Chief when he thought the Chief was going to tell the tale on him as a joke. He'd told it on himself as a penance, in the place of the blow he'd given the Chief and which the Chief wouldn't return. To Mike it was still tragedy. It was still an outrage to his dignity. But Sally was laughing. She rocked back and forth next to Joe, helpless with mirth.

"Oh, Mike!" she gasped. "It's beautiful! They must have been saying such lovely, respectful things, while you were calling them names and wanting to kill them! They'd have been bragging to each other about how you were--visiting them because they'd been such good people, and--this was the reward of well-spent lives, and you--you----"

She leaned against Joe and shook. The car went on. The Chief chuckled. Haney grinned. Joe watched Mike as this new aspect of his disgrace got into his consciousness. It hadn't occurred to Mike, before, that anybody but himself had been ridiculous. It hadn't occurred to him, until he lost his temper, that Haney and the Chief would ride him mercilessly among themselves, but would not dream of letting anybody outside the gang do so.

Presently Mike managed to grin a little. It was a twisty grin, and not altogether mirthful.

"Yeah," he said wrily. "I see it. They were crazy too. I should've had more sense than to get mad." Then his grin grew a trifle twistier. "I didn't tell you that the thing that made me maddest was when they wanted to put earrings on me. I grabbed a club then and--uh--persuaded them I didn't like the idea."

Sally chortled. The picture of the small, truculent Mike in frenzied revolt with a club against the idea of being decked with jewelry.... Mike turned to the two big men and shoved at them imperiously.

"Move over!" he growled. "If you two big lummoxes had dropped in on those crazy goofs instead of me, they'd've thought you were elephants and set you to work hauling logs!"

He squirmed to a seat between them. He still looked ashamed, but it was shame of a different sort. Now he looked as if he wished he hadn't mistrusted his friends for even a moment. And he included Sally.

"Anyhow," he said suddenly in a different tone, "maybe it did do some good for me to get all worked up! I got kind of frantic. I figured somebody'd made a fool of me, and I was going to put something over on you."

"Mike!" said Sally reproachfully.

"Not like you think, Sally," said Mike, grinning a little. "I made up my mind to beat these lummoxes at their own game. I asked Joe about my brainstorm in the plane. He didn't know what I was driving at, but he said what I hoped was so. So I'm telling you--and," he added fiercely, "if it's any good everybody gets credit for it, because all of us four--even two big apes who try kidding--are responsible for it!"

He glared at them. Joe asked. "What is it, Mike?"

"I think," said Mike, "I think I've got a trick to make space ships quicker than anybody ever dreamed of. Joe says you can make a weld with powder metallurgy.

And I think we can use that trick to make one-piece ships--lighter and stronger and tighter--and fast enough to make your head swim! And you guys are in on it!"

The black car braked by the entrance to the Security offices outside the Shed. It looked completely deserted. There was only a skeleton force here since the Platform had been launched three months before. There was almost nobody to be seen, but Mike pressed his lips pugnaciously together as they got out of the car and went inside.

The four of them, with Sally, went along the empty corridors to the major's office. He was waiting for them. He shook hands all around. But it was not possible for Major Holt to give an impression of cordiality.

"I'm very glad to see all of you back," he said curtly. "It didn't look like you'd make it. Joe, you will be able to reach your father by long-distance telephone as soon as you finish here. I--ah--thought it would not be indiscreet to tell him you had landed safely, though I did ask him to keep the fact to himself."

"Thank you, sir," said Joe.

"You answered most of the questions you needed to answer on the plane," added the major, grimly, "and now you may want to ask some. You know there is no ship for you. You know that the enemies of the Platform copied our rocket fuel. You know they've made rockets with it. You've met them! And Intelligence says they're building a fleet of space ships--not for space exploration, but simply to smash the Platform and get set for an ultimatum to the United States to backwater or be bombarded from space."

Mike said crisply: "How long before they can do it?"

Major Holt turned uncordial eyes upon him. "It's anybody's guess. Why?"

"We've been working something out," said Mike, firmly but in part untruthfully. He stood sturdily before the major's desk, which he barely topped. "The four of us have been working it out. Joe says they've done powder metallurgy welds, back at his father's plant. Joe and Haney and the Chief and me, we've been working out an idea."

Major Holt waited. His hands moved nervously on his desk. Joe looked at Mike. Haney and the Chief regarded him warily. The Chief cocked his head on one side.

"It'll take a minute to get it across," said Mike. "You have to think of concrete first. When you want to make a cubic yard of concrete, you take a cubic yard of gravel. Then you add some sand--just enough to fill in the cracks between the grav-el. Then you put in some cement. It goes in the cracks between the grains of sand. A little bit of cement makes a lot of concrete. See?"

Major Holt frowned. But he knew these four. "I see, but I don't understand."

"You can weld metals together with powder-metallurgy powder at less than red heat. You can take steel filings for sand and steel turnings for gravel and pow-dered steel for cement--"

Joe jolted erect. He looked startledly at Haney and the Chief. And Haney's mouth was dropping open. A great, dreamy light seemed to be bursting upon him. The Chief regarded Mike with very bright eyes. And Mike sturdily, forcefully, coldly, made a sort of speech in his small and brittle voice.

Things could be made of solid steel, he said sharply, without rolling or milling or die-casting the metal, and without riveting or arc-welding the parts together. The trick was powder metallurgy. Very finely powdered metal, packed tightly and heated to a relatively low temperature--"sintered" is the word--becomes a solid mass. Even alloys can be made by mixing powdered metals. The process had been used only for small objects, but--there was the analogy to concrete. A very little powder could weld much metal, in the form of turnings and smaller bits. And the result would be solid steel!

Then Mike grew impassioned. There was a wooden mockup of a space ship in the Shed, he said. It was an absolutely accurate replica, in wood, of the ships that had been destroyed. But one could take castings of it, and use them for molds, and fill them with powder and filings and turnings, and heat them not even red-hot and there would be steel hulls in one piece. Solid steel hulls! Needing no riveting nor anything else--and one could do it fast! While the first hull was fitting out a second could be molded----

The Chief roared: "You fool little runt!" he bellowed. "Tryin' to give us credit for that! You got more sense than any of us! You worked that out in your own head-
---"

Haney rubbed his hands together. He said softly, "I like that! I do like that!"

Major Holt turned his eyes to Joe. "What's your opinion?"

"I think it's the sort of thing, sir, that a professional engineer would say was a good idea but not practical. He'd mean it would be a lot of trouble to get working.

But I'd like to ask my father. They have done powder welding at the plant back home, sir."

Major Holt nodded. "Call your father. If it looks promising, I'll pull what wires I can."

Joe went out, with the others. Mike was sweating. All unconsciously, he twisted his hands one within the other. He had had many humiliations because he was small, but lately he had humiliated himself by not believing in his friends. Now he needed desperately to do something that would reflect credit on them as well as himself.

Joe made the phone call. As he closed the door of the booth, he heard the Chief kidding Mike blandly.

"Hey, Einstein," said the Chief. "How about putting that brain of yours to work on a faster-than-light drive?"

But then he began to struggle with the long distance operator. It took minutes to get the plant, and then it took time to get to the point, because his father insisted on asking anxiously how he was and if he was hurt in any way. Personal stuff. But Joe finally managed to explain that this call dealt with the desperate need to do something about a space fleet.

His father said grimly, "Yes. The situation doesn't look too good right now, Joe."

"Try this on for size, sir," said Joe. He outlined Mike's scheme. His father interrupted only to ask crisp questions about the mockup of the tender, already in existence though made of wood. Then he said, "Go on, son!"

Joe finished. He heard his father speaking to someone away from the phone. Questions and answers, and then orders. His father spoke to him direct.

"It looks promising, Joe," said his father. "Right here at the plant we've got the gang that can do it if anybody can. I'm getting a plane and coming out there, fast! Get Major Holt to clear things for me. This is no time for red tape! If he has trouble, I'll pull some wires myself!"

"Then I can tell Mike it's good stuff?"

"It's not good stuff," said his father. "There are about forty-seven things wrong with it at first glance, but I know how to take care of one or two, and we'll lick the rest. You tell your friend Mike I want to shake him by the hand. I hope to do it tonight!"

He hung up, and Joe went out of the phone booth. Mike looked at him with yearning eyes. Joe lied a little, because Mike rated it.

"My father's on the way here to help make it work," he told Mike. Then he added untruthfully: "He said he thought he knew all the big men in his line, and where've you been that he hasn't heard of you?"

He turned away as the Chief whooped with glee. He hurried back to Major Holt as the Chief and Haney began zestfully to manhandle Mike in celebration of his genius.

The major held up his hand as Joe entered. He was using the desk phone. Joe waited. When he hung up, Joe reported. The major seemed unsurprised.

"Yes, I had Washington on the wire," he said detachedly. "I talked to a personal friend who's a three-star general. There will be action started at the Pentagon. When you came in I was arranging with the largest producers of powder-metallurgy products in the country to send their best men here by plane. They will start at once. Now I have to get in touch with some other people."

Joe gaped at him. The major moved impatiently, waiting for Joe to leave. Joe gulped. "Excuse me, sir, but--my father didn't say it was certain. He just thinks it can be made to work. He's not sure."

"I didn't even wait for that, something has to turn up to take care of this situation!" said the Major with asperity. "It has to! This particular scheme may not work, but if it doesn't, something will come out of the work on it! You should look at a twenty-five cent piece occasionally, Joe!"

He moved impatiently, and Joe went out. Sally was smiling in the outer office. There were whoopings in the corridor beyond. The Chief and Haney were celebrating Mike's brainstorm with salutary indignity, because if they didn't make a joke of it he might cry with joy.

"Things look better?"

"They do," said Joe. "If it only works...."

Then he hunted in his pocket. He found a quarter and examined it curiously. On one side he found nothing the major could have referred to. On the other side, though, just by George Washington's chin----

He put the quarter away and took Sally's arm.

"It'll be all right," he said slowly.

But there were times when it seemed in doubt. Joe's father arrived by plane at sunset of that same day, and he and three men from the Kenmore Precision Tool Company instantly closeted themselves with Mike in Major Holt's quarters. The powder metallurgy men turned up an hour later, and a three-star general from Washington. They joined the highly technical discussion.

Joe waited around outside, feeling left out of things. He sat on the porch with Sally while the moon rose over the desert and stars shone down. Inside, matters of high importance were being battled over with the informality and heat with which practical men get things settled. But Joe wasn't in on it. He said annoyedly, "You'd think my father'd have something to say to me, in all this mess! After all, I have been--well, I have been places! But all he said was, 'How are you, Son? Where's this Mike you talked about?'"

Sally said calmly, "I know just how you feel. You've made me feel that way." She looked up at the moon. "I thought about you all the time you were gone, and I--prayed for you, Joe. And now you're back and not even busy! But you don't---- It would be nice for you to think about me for a while!"

"I am thinking about you!" said Joe indignantly.

"Now what," said Sally interestedly, "in the world could you be thinking about me?"

He wanted to scowl at her. But he grinned instead.

7

Time passed. Hours, then days. Things began to happen. Trucks appeared, loaded down with sacks of white powder. The powder was very messily mixed with water and smeared lavishly over the now waterproofed wooden mockup of a space ship. It came off again in sections of white plaster, which were numbered and set to dry in warm chambers that were constructed with almost magical speed. More trucks arrived, bearing such diverse objects as loads of steel turnings, a regenerative helium-cooling plant from a gaswell--it could cool metal down to the point where it crumbled to impalpable powder at a blow--and assorted fuel tanks, dynamos, and electronic machinery.

Ten days after Mike's first proposal of concreted steel as a material for space ship construction, the parts of the first casting of the mockup were assembled. They were a mold for the hull of a space ship. There were more plaster sections for a second mold ready to be dried out now, but meanwhile vehicles like concrete mixers mixed turnings and filings and powder in vast quantities and poured the dry mass here and there in the first completed mold. Then men began to wrap the gigantic object with iron wire. Presently that iron wire glowed slightly, and the whole huge mold grew hotter and hotter and hotter. And after a time it was allowed to cool.

But that did not mean a ceasing of activity. The plaster casts had been made while the concreting process was worked out. The concreting process--including the heating--was in action while fittings were being flown to the Shed. But other hulls were being formed by metal-concrete formation even before the first mold was taken down.

When the plaster sections came off, there was a long, gleaming, frosty-sheened metal hull waiting for the fittings. It was a replacement of one of the two shot-down space craft, ready for fitting out some six weeks ahead of schedule. Next day there was a second metal hull, still too hot to touch. The day after that there was another.

Then they began to be turned out at the rate of two a day, and all the vast expanse of the Shed resounded with the work on them. Drills drilled and torches burned and hammers hammered. Small diesels rumbled. Disk saws cut metal like butter by the seemingly impractical method of spinning at 20,000 revolutions per minute. Convoys of motor busses rolled out from Bootstrap at change-shift time, and there were again Security men at every doorway, moving continually about.

But it still didn't look too good. There is apparently no way to beat arithmetic, and a definitely grim problem still remained. Ten days after the beginning of the new construction program, Joe and Sally looked down from a gallery high up in the outward-curving wall of the Shed. Acres of dark flooring lay beneath them. There was a spiral ramp that wound round and round between the twin skins of the fifty-story-high dome. It led finally to the Communications Room at the very top of the Shed itself.

Where Joe and Sally looked down, the floor was 300 feet below. Welding arcs glittered. Rivet guns chattered. Trucks came in the doorways with materials, and there was already a gleaming row of eighty-foot hulls. There were eleven of them already uncovered, and small trucks ran up to their sides to feed the fitting-out crews such items as air tanks and gyro assemblies and steering rocket piping and motors, and short wave communicators and control boards. Exit doors were being fitted. The last two hulls to be uncovered were being inspected with portable x-ray outfits, in search of flaws. And there were still other ungainly white molds, which were other hulls in process of formation--the metal still pouring into the molds in powder form, or being tamped down, or being sintered to solidity.

Joe leaned on the gallery-railing and said unhappily, "I can't help worrying, even though the Platform hasn't been shot at since we landed."

That wasn't an expression of what he was thinking. He was thinking about matters the enemies of the Platform would have liked to know about. Sally knew these matters too. But top secret information isn't talked about by the people who know it, unless they are actively at work on it. At all other times one pretends even to himself that he doesn't know it. That is the only possible way to avoid leaks.

The top secret information was simply that it was still impossible to supply the Platform. Ships could be made faster than had ever been dreamed of before, but so long as any ship that went up could be destroyed on the way down, the supply of the Platform was impractical. But the ships were being built regardless, against the time when a way to get them down again was thought of. As of the moment it hadn't been thought of yet.

But building the ships anyhow was unconscious genius, because nobody but Americans could imagine anything so foolish. The enemies of the Platform and of the United States knew that full-scale production of ships by some fantastic new method was in progress. The fact couldn't be hidden. But nobody in a country where material shortages were chronic could imagine building ships before a way to use them was known. So the Platform's enemies were convinced that the United States had something wholly new and very remarkable, and threatened their spies with unspeakable fates if they didn't find out what it was.

They didn't find out. The rulers of the enemy nations knew, of course, that if a new--say--space-drive had been invented, they would very soon have to change their tune. So there were no more attacks on the Platform. It floated serenely overhead, sending down astronomical observations and solar-constant measurements and weather maps, while about it floated a screen of garbage and discarded tin cans.

But Joe and Sally looked down where the ships were being built while the problem of how to use them was debated.

"It's a tough nut to crack," said Joe dourly.

It haunted him. Ships going up had to have crews. Crews had to come down again because they had to leave supplies at the Platform, not consume them there. Getting a ship up to orbit was easier than getting it down again.

"The Navy's been working on light guided missiles," said Sally.

"No good," snapped Joe.

It wasn't. He'd been asked for advice. Could a space ship crew control guided missiles and fight its way back to ground with them? The answer was that it could. But guided missiles used to fight one's way down would have to be carried up first. And they would weigh as much as all the cargo a ship could carry. A ship that carried fighting rockets couldn't carry cargo. Cargo at the Platform was the thing desired.

"All that's needed," said Sally, watching Joe's face, "is a slight touch of genius. There's been genius before now. Burning your cabin free with landing-rocket flames----"

"Haney's idea," growled Joe dispiritedly.

"And making more ships in a hurry with metal-concrete----"

"Mike did that," said Joe ruefully.

"But you made the garbage-screen for the Platform," insisted Sally.

"Sanford had made a wisecrack," said Joe. "And it just happened that it made sense that he hadn't noticed." He grimaced. "You say something like that, now...."

Sally looked at him with soft eyes. It wasn't really his job, this worrying. The top-level brains of the armed forces were struggling with it. They were trying everything from redesigned rocket motors to really radical notions. But there wasn't anything promising yet.

"What's really needed," said Sally regretfully, "is a way for ships to go up to the Platform and not have to come back."

"Sure!" said Joe ironically. Then he said, "Let's go down!"

They started down the long, winding ramp which led between the two skins of the Shed's wall. It was quite empty, this long, curving, descending corridor. It was remarkably private. In a place like the Shed, with frantic activity going on all around, and even at Major Holt's quarters where Sally lived and Joe was a guest, there wasn't often a chance for them to talk in any sort of actual privacy.

But Joe went on, scowling. Sally went with him. If she seemed to hang back a little at first, he didn't notice. Presently she shrugged her shoulders and ceased to try to make him notice that nobody else happened to be around. They made a complete circuit of the Shed within its wall, Joe staring ahead without words.

Then he stopped abruptly. His expression was unbelieving. Sally almost bumped into him.

"What's the matter?"

"You had it, Sally!" he said amazedly. "You did it! You said it!"

"What?"

"The touch of genius!" He almost babbled. "Ships that can go up to the Platform and not have to come back! Sally, you did it! You did it!"

She regarded him helplessly. He took her by the shoulders as if to shake her into comprehension. But he kissed her exuberantly instead.

"Come on!" he said urgently. "I've got to tell the gang!"

He grabbed her hand and set off at a run for the bottom of the ramp. And Sally, with remarkably mingled emotions showing on her face, was dragged in his wake.

He was still pulling her after him when he found the Chief and Haney and Mike in the room at Security where they were practically self-confined, lest their return to Earth become too publicly known. Mike was stalking up and down with his hands clasped behind his back, glum as a miniature Napoleon and talking bitterly. The Chief was sprawled in a chair. Haney sat upright regarding his knuckles with a thoughtful air.

Joe stepped inside the door. Mike continued without a pause: "I tell you, if they'll only use little guys like me, the cabin and supplies and crew can be cut down by tons! Even the instruments can be smaller and weigh less! Four of us in a smaller cabin, less grub and air and water--we'll save tons in cabin-weight alone! Why can't you big lummoxes see it?"

"We see it, Mike," Haney said mildly. "You're right. But people won't do it. It's not fair, but they won't."

Joe said, beaming, "Besides, Mike, it'd bust up our gang! And Sally's just gotten the real answer! The answer is for ships to go up to the Platform and not come back!"

He grinned at them. The Chief raised his eyebrows. Haney turned his head to stare. Joe said exuberantly: "They've been talking about arming ships with guided missiles to fight with. Too heavy, of course. But--if we could handle guided missiles, why couldn't we handle drones?"

The three of them gaped at him. Sally said, startled, "But--but, Joe, I didn't----"

"We've got plenty of hulls!" said Joe. Somehow he still looked astonished at what he'd made of Sally's perfectly obvious comment. "Mike's arranged for that! Make--say--six of 'em into drones--space barges. Remote-controlled ships. Control them from one manned ship--the tug! We'll ride that! Take 'em up to the Platform exactly like a tug tows barges. The tow-line will be radio beams. We'll have a space-tow up, and not bother to bring the barges back! There won't be any landing rockets! They'll carry double cargo! That's the answer! A space tug hauling a tow to the Platform!"

"But, Joe," insisted Sally, "I didn't think of----"

The Chief heaved himself up. Haney's voice cut through what the Chief was about to say. Haney said drily: "Sally, if Joe hadn't kissed you for thinking that up, I would. Makes me feel mighty dumb."

Mike swallowed. Then he said loyally, "Yeah. Me too. I'd've made a two-ton cargo possible--maybe. But this adds up. What does the major say?"

"I--haven't talked to him. I'd better, right away." Joe grinned. "I wanted to tell you first."

The Chief grunted. "Good idea. But hold everything!" He fumbled in his pocket. "The arithmetic is easy enough, Joe. Cut out the crew and air and you save something." He felt in another pocket. "Leave off the landing rockets, and you save plenty more. Count in the cargo you could take anyhow"---- he searched another pocket still----"and you get forty-two tons of cargo per space barge, delivered at the Platform. Six drones--that's 252 tons in one tow! Here!" He'd found what he wanted. It was a handkerchief. He thrust it upon Joe. "Wipe that lipstick off, Joe, before you go talk to the major. He's Sally's father and he might not like it."

Joe wiped at his face. Sally, her eyes shining, took the handkerchief from him and finished the job. She displayed that remarkable insensitivity of females in situations productive of both pride and embarrassment. When a girl or a woman is proud, she is never embarrassed.

She and Joe went away, and Sally rushed right into her father's office. In fifteen minutes technical men began to arrive for conferences, summoned by telephone. Within forty-five minutes, messengers carried orders out to the Shed floor and stopped the installation of certain types of fittings in all but one of the hulls. In an hour and a half, top technical designers were doing the work of foremen and getting things done without benefit of blueprints. The proposal was beautifully simple to put into practice. Guided-missile control systems were already in mass production. They could simply be adjusted to take care of drones.

Within twelve hours there were truck-loads of new sorts of supplies arriving at the Shed. Some were Air Force supplies and some were Ordnance, and some were strictly Quartermaster. These were not component parts of space ships. They were freight for the Platform.

And, just forty-eight hours after Joe and Sally looked dispiritedly down upon the floor of the Shed, there were seven gleaming hulls in launching cages and the unholy din of landing pushpots outside the Shed. They came with hysterical cries from their airfield to the south, and they flopped flat with extravagant crashings on the desert outside the eastern door.

By the time the pushpots had been hauled in, one by one, and had attached themselves to the launching cages, Joe and Haney and the Chief and Mike had climbed into the cabin of the one ship which was not a drone. There were now seven cages in all to be hoisted toward the sky. A great double triangular gore had been jacked out and rolled aside to make an exit in the side of the Shed. Nearly as many pushpots, it seemed, were involved in this launching as in the take-off of the Platform itself.

The routine test before take-off set the pushpot motors to roaring inside the Shed. The noise was the most sustained and ghastly tumult that had been heard on Earth since the departure of the Platform.

But this launching was not so impressive. It was definitely untidy, imprecise, and unmilitary. There were seven eighty-foot hulls in cages surrounded by clustering, bellowing, preposterous groups of howling objects that looked like over-sized black beetles. One of the seven hulls had eyes. The others were blind--but they were equipped with radio antennae. The ship with eyes had several small basket-type radar bowls projecting from its cabin plating.

The seven objects rose one by one and went bellowing and blundering out to the open air. At 40 and 50 feet above the ground, they jockeyed into some sort of formation, with much wallowing and pitching and clumsy maneuvering.

Then, without preliminary, they started up. They rose swiftly. The noise of their going diminished from a bellow to a howl, and from a howl to a moaning noise, and then to a faint, faint, ever-dwindling hum.

Presently that faded out, too.

8

All the sensations were familiar, the small fleet of improbable objects rose and rose. Of all flying objects ever imagined by man, the launching cages supported by pushpots were most irrational.

The squadron, though, went bumbling upward. In the manned ship, Joe was more tense than on his other take-off--if such a thing was possible. His work was harder this trip. Before, he'd had Mike at communications and the Chief at the steering rockets while Haney kept the pushpots balanced for thrust. Now Joe flew the manned ship alone. Headphones and a mike gave him communications with the Shed direct, and the pushpots were balanced in groups, which cost efficiency but helped on control. He would have, moreover, to handle his own steering rockets during acceleration and when he could--and dared--he should supervise the others. Because each of the other three had two drone-ships to guide. True, they had only to keep their drones in formation, but Joe had to navigate for all. The four of them had been assigned this flight because of its importance. They happened to be the only crew alive who had ever flown a space ship designed for maneuvering, and their experience consisted of a single trip.

The jet stream was higher this time than on that other journey now two months past. They blundered into it at 36,000 feet. Joe's headphones buzzed tinnily. Radar from the ground told him his rate-of-rise, his ground speed, his orbital speed, and added comments on the handling of the drones.

The last was not a precision job. On the way up Joe protested, "Somebody's ship--Number Four--is lagging! Snap it up!"

Mike said crisply, "Got it, Joe. Coming up!"

"The Shed says three separate ships are getting out of formation. And we need due east pointing. Check it."

The Chief muttered, "Something whacky here ... come round, you! Okay, Joe."

Joe had no time for reflection. He was in charge of the clumsiest operation ever designed for an exact result. The squadron went wallowing toward the sky. The noise was horrible. A tinny voice in his headphones:

"You are at 65,000 feet. Your rate-of-climb curve is flattening. You should fire your jatos when practical. You have some leeway in rocket power."

Joe spoke into the extraordinary maze of noise waves and pressure systems in the air of the cabin.

"We should blast. I'm throwing in the series circuit for jatos. Try to line up. We want the drones above us and with a spread, remember! Go to it!"

He watched his direction indicator and the small graphic indicators telling of the drones. The sky outside the ports was dark purple. The launching cage responded sluggishly. Its open end came around toward the east. It wobbled and wavered. It touched the due-east point. Joe stabbed the firing-button.

Nothing happened. He hadn't expected it. The seven ships had to keep in formation. They had to start off on one course--with a slight spread as a safety measure--and at one time. So the firing-circuits were keyed to relays in series. Only when all seven firing-keys were down at the same time would any of the jatos fire. Then all would blast together.

The pilots in the cockpit-bubbles of the pushpots had an extraordinary view of the scene. At something over twelve miles height, seven aggregations of clumsy black things clung to frameworks of steel, pushing valorously. Far below there were clouds and there was Earth. There was a horizon, which wavered and tilted. The pushpots struggled with seeming lack of purpose. One of the seven seemed to drop below the others. They pointed vaguely this way and that--all of them. But gradually they seemed to arrive at an uncertain unanimity.

Joe pushed the firing-button again as his own ship touched the due-east mark. Again nothing happened. Out of the corner of his eye he saw Haney pressing down both buttons. The Chief's finger lifted. Mike pushed down one button and held off the other.

Roarings and howlings of pushpots. Wobblings and heart-breaking clumsinesses of the drone-ships. They hung in the sky while the pushpots used up their fuel.

"We've got to make it soon," said Joe grimly. "We've got forty seconds. Or we'll have to go down and try again."

There was a clock dial with a red sweep-hand which moved steadily and ominously toward a deadline time for firing. Up to that deadline, the pushpots could let the ships back down to Earth without crashing them. After it, they'd run out of fuel before a landing could be made.

The deadline came closer and closer. Joe snapped:

"Take a degree leeway. We've got ten seconds."

He had the manned ship nearly steady. He held down the firing-button, holding aim by infinitesimal movements of the controls. Haney pushed both hands down, raised one, pushed again. The Chief had one finger down. Mike had both firing buttons depressed.... The Chief pushed down his second button, quietly.

There was a monstrous impact. Every jato in every pushpot about every launching cage fired at once. Joe felt himself flung back into his acceleration chair. Six gravities. He began the horrible fight to stay alive, while the blood tried to drain from the conscious forepart of his brain, and while every button of his garments pressed noticeably against him, and objects in his pockets pushed. The sides of his mouth dragged back, and his cheeks sagged, and his tongue strove to sink back into his throat and strangle him.

It was very bad. It seemed to last for centuries.

Then the jatos burned out. There was that ghastly feeling of lunging forward to weightlessness. One instant, Joe's body weighed half a ton. The next instant, it weighed less than a dust grain. His head throbbed twice as if his skull were about to split open and let his brains run out. But these things he had experienced before.

There were pantings in the cabin about him. The ship fell. It happened to be going up, but the sensation and the fact was free fall. Joe had been through this before, too. He gasped for breath and croaked, "Drones?"

"Right," said Haney.

Mike panted anxiously, "Four's off course. I'll fix it."

The Chief grunted guttural Mohawk. His hands stirred on the panel for remote control of the drones he had to handle.

"Crazy!" he growled. "Got it now, Joe. Fire when ready."

"Okay, Mike?"

A half-second pause.

"Okay!"

Joe pressed the firing-button for the take-off rockets. And he was slammed back into his acceleration chair again. But this was three gravities only. Pressed heavily against the acceleration cushions, he could perform the navigation for the fleet. He did. The mother-ship had to steer a true course, regardless of the vagaries of its rockets. The drones had simply to be kept in formation with it. The second task was simpler. But Joe was relieved, this time, of the need to report back instrument-readings. A telemetering device took care of that.

The take-off rockets blasted and blasted and blasted. The mere matter of staying alive grew very tedious. The ordeal seemed to last for centuries. Actually it could be measured only in minutes. But it seemed millennia before the headphones said, staccato fashion: "*You are on course and will reach speed in fourteen seconds. I will count for you.*"

"Relays for rocket release," panted Joe. "Throw 'em over!"

Three hands moved to obey. Joe could release the drive rockets on all seven ships at will.

The voice counted:

"*Ten ... nine ... eight ... seven ... six ... five ... four ... three ... two ... one ... cut!*"

Joe pressed the master-key. The remnants of the solid-fuel take-off rockets let go. They flashed off into nothingness at unbelievable speed, consuming themselves as they went.

There was again no weight.

This time there was no resting. No eager gazing out the cabin ports. Now they weren't curious. They'd had over a month in space, and something like sixteen days back on Earth, and now they were back in space again.

Mike and Haney and the Chief worked doggedly at their control boards. The radar bowls outside the cabin shifted and moved and quivered. The six drone ships showed on the screens. But they also had telemetering apparatus. They faithfully reported their condition and the direction in which their bows pointed. The radars plotted their position with relation to each other and the mother-ship.

Presently Joe cast a glance out of a port and saw that the dark line of sunset was almost below. The take-off had been timed to get the ships into Earth's shadow above the area from which war rockets were most likely to rise. It wouldn't prevent bombing, of course. But there was a gadget....

Joe spoke into the microphone: "Reporting everything all right so far. But you know it."

The voice from solid ground said, "***Report acknowledged.***"

The ships went on and on and on. The Chief muttered to himself and made very minute adjustments of the movement of one of his drones. Mike fussed with his. Haney regarded the controls of his drones with a profound calm.

Nothing happened, except that they seemed to be falling into a bottomless pit and their stomach-muscles knotted and cramped in purely reflex response to the sensation. Even that grew tedious.

The headphones said, "***You will enter Earth's shadow in three minutes. Prepare for combat.***"

Joe said drily, "We're to prepare for combat."

The Chief growled. "I'd like to do just that!"

The phrasing, of course, was intentional--in case enemy ears were listening. Actually, the small fleet was to use a variant on the tin can shield which protected the Platform. It would be most effective if visual observation was impossible. The fleet was seven ships in very ragged formation. Most improbably, after the long three-gravity acceleration, they were still within a fifty-mile globe of space. Number Four loitered behind, but was being brought up by judicious bursts of steering-rocket fire. Number Two was some distance ahead. The others were simply scattered. They went floating on like a group of meteors. Out the ports, two of them were visible. The others might be picked out by the naked eye--but it wasn't likely.

Drone Two, far ahead and clearly visible, turned from a shining steel speck to a reddish pin-point of light. The red color deepened. It winked out. The sunlight in the ports of the mother-ship turned red. Then it blacked out.

"Shoot the ghosts," said Joe.

The three drone-handlers pushed their buttons. Nothing happened that anybody could see. Actually, though, a small gadget outside the hull began to cough rhythmically. Similar devices on the drones coughed, too. They were small, multiple-barreled guns. Rifle shells fired two-pound missiles at random targets in emptiness. They wouldn't damage anything they hit. They'd go varying distances, explode and shoot small lead shot ahead to check their missile-velocity, and then emit dense masses of aluminum foil. There was no air resistance. The shredded foil would continue to move through emptiness at the same rate as the convoy-fleet. The seven ships had fired a total of eighty-four such objects away into the blackness of Earth's shadow. There were, then, seven ships and eighty-four masses of aluminum foil moving through emptiness. They could not be seen by telescopes.

And radars could not tell ships from masses of aluminum foil.

If enemy radars came probing upward, they reported ninety-one space ships in ragged but coherent formation, soaring through emptiness toward the Platform. And a fleet like that was too strong to attack.

The radar operators had been prepared to forward details of the speed and course of a single ship to waiting rocket-launching submarines half-way across the Pacific. But they reported to Very High Authority instead.

He received the report of an armada--an incredible fleet--in space. He didn't believe it. But he didn't dare disbelieve it.

So the fleet swam peacefully through the darkness that was Earth's shadow, and no attempt at attack was made. They came out into sunlight to look down at the western shore of America itself. With seven ships to get on an exact course, at an exact speed, at an exact moment, time was needed. So the fleet made almost a complete circuit of the Earth before reaching the height of the Platform's orbit.

They joined it. A single man in a space suit, anchored to its outer plates, directed a plastic hose which stretched out impossibly far and clamped to one drone with a magnetic grapple. He maneuvered it to the hull and made it fast. He captured a second, which was worked delicately within reach by coy puffs of steering-rocket vapor.

One by one, the drones were made fast. Then the manned ship went in the lock and the great outer door closed, and the plastic-fabric walls collapsed behind their nets, and air came in.

Lieutenant Commander Brown was the one to come into the lock to greet them. He shook hands all around--and it again seemed strange to all the four from Earth to find themselves with their feet more or less firmly planted on a solid floor, but their bodies wavering erratically to right and left and before and back, because there was no up or down.

"Just had reports from Earth," Brown told Joe comfortably. "The news of your take-off was released to avoid panic in Europe. But everybody who doesn't like us is yelling blue murder. Somebody--you may guess who--is announcing that a fleet of ninety-one war rockets took off from the United States and now hangs poised in space while the decadent American war-mongers prepare an ultimatum to all the world. Everybody's frightened."

"If they'll only stay scared until we get unloaded," said Joe in some satisfaction, "the government back home can tell them how many we were and what we came up for. But we'll probably make out all right, anyhow."

"My crew will unload," said Brown, in conscious thoughtfulness. "You must have gotten pretty well exhausted by that acceleration."

Joe shook his head. "I think we can handle the freight faster. We found out a few things by going back to Earth."

A section of plating at the top of the lock--at least it had been the top when the Platform was built on Earth--opened up as on the first journey here. A face grinned down. But from this point on, the procedure was changed. Haney and Joe went into the cargo-section of the rocketship and heaved its contents smoothly through weightlessness to the storage chamber above. The Chief and Mike stowed it there. The speed and precision of their work was out of all reason. Brown stared incredulously.

The fact was simply that on their first trip to the Platform, Joe and his crew didn't know how to use their strength where there was no weight. By the time they'd learned, their muscles had lost all tone. Now they were fresh from Earth, with Earth-strength muscles--and they knew how to use them.

"When we got back," Joe told Brown, "we were practically invalids. No exercise up here. This time we've brought some harness to wear. We've some for you, too."

They moved out of the airlock, and the ship was maneuvered to a mooring outside, and a drone took its place. Brown's eyes blinked at the unloading of the drone. But he said, "Navy style work, that!"

"Out here," said Joe, "you take no more exercise than an invalid on Earth--in fact, not as much. By now the original crew would have trouble standing up on a trip back to Earth. You'd feel pretty heavy, yourself."

Brown frowned.

"Hm. I--ah--I shall ask for instructions on the matter."

He stood erect. He didn't waver on his feet as the others did. But he wore the same magnetic-soled shoes. Joe knew, with private amusement, that Brown must have worked hard to get a dignified stance in weightlessness.

"Mr. Kenmore," said Brown suddenly. "Have you been assigned a definite rank as yet?"

"Not that I know of," said Joe without interest. "I skipper the ship I just brought up. But----"

"Your ship has no rating!" protested Brown irritably. "The skipper of a Navy ship may be anything from a lieutenant junior grade to a captain, depending on the size and rating of the ship. In certain circumstances even a noncommissioned officer. Are you an enlisted man?"

"Again, not that I know of," Joe told him. "Nor my crew, either."

Brown looked at once annoyed and distressed.

"It isn't regular!" he objected. "It isn't shipshape! I should know whether you are under my command or not! For discipline! For organization! It should be cleared up! I shall put through an urgent inquiry."

Joe looked at him incredulously. Lieutenant Commander Brown was a perfectly amiable man, but he had to have things in a certain pattern for him to recognize that they were in a pattern at all. He was more excited over the fact that he didn't know whether he ranked Joe, than over the much more important matter of physical deterioration in the absence of gravity. Yet he surely understood their relative importance. The fact was, of course, that he could confidently expect exact instructions about the last, while he had to settle matters of discipline and routine for himself.

"I shall ask for clarification of your status," he said worriedly. "It shouldn't have been left unclear. I'd better attend to it at once."

He looked at Joe as if expecting a salute. He didn't get it. He clanked away, his magnetic shoe-soles beating out a singularly martial rhythm. He must have practised that walk, in private.

Joe got out of the airlock as another of the space barges was warped in. Brent, the crew's psychologist, joined him when he went to unload. Brent nodded in a friendly fashion to Joe.

"Quite a change, eh?" he said drily. "Sanford turned out to be a crackpot with his notions of grandeur. I'm not sure that Brown's notions of discipline aren't worse."

Joe said, "I've something rather important to pass on," and told about the newly discovered physical effects of a long stay where there was no gravity. The doctors now predicted that anybody who spent six months without weight would suffer a deterioration of muscle tone which could make a return to Earth impossible without a long preliminary process of retraining. One's heart would adjust to the absence of any need to pump blood against gravity.

"Which," said Joe, "means that you're going to have to be relieved before too long. But we brought up some gravity-simulator harness that may help."

Brent said desolately: "And I was so pleased! We all had trouble with insomnia, at first, but lately we've all been sleeping well! Now I see why! Normally one sleeps because he's tired. We had trouble sleeping until our muscles got so weak we tired anyhow!"

Another drone came in and was unloaded. And another and another. But the last of them wasn't only unloaded. Haney took over the Platform's control board and--grinning to himself--sent faint, especially-tuned short wave impulses to the steering-rockets of the drone. The liquid-fuel rockets were designed to steer a loaded ship. With the airlock door open, the silvery ship leaped out of the dock like a frightened horse. The liquid-fuel rocket had a nearly empty hull to accelerate. It responded skittishly.

Joe watched out a port as it went hurtling away. The vast Earth rolled beneath it. It sped on and vanished. Its fumes ceased to be visible. Joe told Brent:

"Another nice job, that! We sent it backward, slowing it a little. It'll have a new orbit, independent of ours and below it. But come sixty hours it will be directly underneath. We'll haul it up and refuel it. And our friends the enemy will hate it. It's a radio repeater. It'll pick up short-wave stuff beamed to it, and repeat it down to Earth. And they can try to jam that!"

It was a mildly malicious trick to play. Behind the Iron Curtain, broadcasts from the free world couldn't be heard because of stations built to emit pure noise and drown them out. But the jamming stations were on the enemy nations' borders. If radio programs came down from overhead, jamming would be ineffective at least in the center of the nations. Populations would hear the truth, even though their governments objected.

But that was a minor matter, after all. With space ship hulls coming into being by dozens, and with one convoy of hundreds of tons of equipment gotten aloft, the whole picture of supply for the Platform had changed.

Part of the new picture was two devices that Haney and the Chief were assembling. They were mostly metal backbone and a series of tanks, with rocket motors mounted on ball and socket joints. They looked like huge red insects, but they were officially rocket recovery vehicles, and Joe's crew referred to them as space wagons. They had no cabin, but something like a saddle. Before it there was a control-board complete with radar-screens. And there were racks to which solid-fuel rockets of divers sizes could be attached. They were literally short-range tow craft for travel in space. They had the stripped, barren look of farm machinery. So the name "space wagon" fitted. There were two of them.

"We're putting the pair together," the Chief told Joe. "Looks kinda peculiar."

"It's only for temporary use," said Joe. "There's a bigger and better one being built with a regular cabin and hull. But some experience with these two will be useful in running a regular space tug."

The Chief said with a trace too much of casualness: "I'm kind of looking forward to testing this."

"No," said Joe doggedly. "I'm responsible. I take the first chance. But we should all be able to handle them. When this is assembled you can stand by with the second one. If the first one works all right, we'll try the second."

The Chief grimaced, but he went back to the assembly of the spidery device.

Joe got out the gravity-simulator harnesses. He showed Brent how they worked. Brown hadn't official instructions to order their use, but Joe put one on himself, set for full Earth-gravity simulation. He couldn't imitate actual gravity, of course. Only the effect of gravity on one's muscles. There were springs and elastic webbing pulling one's shoulders and feet together, so that it was as much effort to stand extended--with one's legs straight out--as to stand upright on Earth. Joe felt better with a pull on his body.

Brent was upset when he found that to him more than a tenth of normal gravity was unbearable. But he kept it on at that. If he increased the pull a very little every day, he might be able to return to Earth, in time. Now it would be a very dangerous business indeed. He went off to put the other members of the crew in the same sort of harness.

After ten hours, a second drone broadcaster went off into space. By that time the articulated red frameworks were assembled. They looked more than ever like farm machinery, save that their bulging tanks made them look insectile, too. They were actually something between small tow-boats and crash-wagons. A man in a space suit could climb into the saddle of one of these creations, plug in the air-line of his suit to the crash-wagon's tanks, and travel in space by means of the space wagon's rockets. These weird vehicles had remarkably powerful magnetic grapples. They were equipped with steering rockets as powerful as those of a ship. They had banks of solid-fuel rockets of divers power and length of burning. And they even mounted rocket missiles, small guided rockets which could be used to destroy what could not be recovered. They were intended to handle unmanned rocket shipments of supplies to the Platform. There were reasons why the trick should be economical, if it should happen to work at all.

When they were ready for testing, they seemed very small in the great space lock. Joe and the Chief very carefully checked an extremely long list of things that had to work right or nothing would work at all. That part of the job wasn't thrilling, but Joe no longer looked for thrills. He painstakingly did the things that produced results. If a sense of adventure seemed to disappear, the sensations of achievement more than made up for it.

They got into space suits. They were in an odd position on the Platform. Lieutenant Commander Brown had avoided Joe as much as possible since his arrival. So far he'd carefully avoided giving him direct orders, because Joe was not certainly and officially his subordinate. Lacking exact information, the only thing a conscientious rank-conscious naval officer could do was exercise the maximum of tact and insistently ask authority for a ruling on Joe's place in the hierarchy of rank.

Joe flung a leg over his eccentric, red-painted mount. He clipped his safety-belt, plugged in his suit air-supply to the space wagon's tanks, and spoke into his helmet transmitter.

"Okay to open the lock. Chief, you keep watch. If I make out all right, you can join me. If I get in serious trouble, come after me in the ship we rode up. But only if it's practical! Not otherwise!"

The Chief said something in Mohawk. He sounded indignant.

The plastic walls of the lock swelled inward, burying and overwhelming them. Pumps pounded briefly, removing what air was left. Then the walls drew back, straining against their netting, and Joe waited for the door to open to empty space.

Instead, there came a sharp voice in his helmet-phones. It was Brown. "***Radar says there's a rocket on the way up! It's over at what is the edge of the world from here. Three gravities only. Better not go out!***"

Joe hesitated. Brown still issued no order. But defense against a single rocket would be a matter of guided missiles--Brown's business--if the tin can screen didn't handle it. Joe would have no part in it. He wouldn't be needed. He couldn't help. And there'd be all the elaborate business of checking to go through again. He said uncomfortably:

"It'll be a long time before it gets here--and three gravities is low! Maybe it's a defective job. There have been misfires and so on. It won't take long to try this wagon, anyhow. They're anxious to send up a robot ship from the Shed and these have to be tested first. Give me ten minutes."

He heard the Chief grumbling to himself. But one tested space wagon was better than none.

The airlock doors opened. Huge round valves swung wide. Bright, remote, swarming stars filled the opening. Joe cracked the control of his forward liquid-fuel rockets. The lock filled instantly with swirling fumes. And instantly the tiny space wagon moved. It did not have to lift from the lock floor. Once the magnetic clamps were released it was free of the floor. But it did have mass. One brief push of the rockets sent it floating out of the lock. It was in space. It kept on.

Joe felt a peculiar twinge of panic. Nobody who is accustomed only to Earth can quite realize at the beginning the conditions of handling vehicles in space. But Joe cracked the braking rockets. He stopped. He hung seemingly motionless in space. The Platform was a good half-mile away.

He tried the gyros, and the space wagon went into swift spinning. He reversed them and straightened out--almost. The vastness of all creation seemed still to revolve slowly about him. The monstrous globe which was Earth moved sedately from above his head to under his feet and continued the slow revolution. The Platform rotated in a clockwise direction. He was drifting very slowly away.

"Chief," he said wrily, "you can't do worse than I'm doing, and we're rushed for time. You might come out. But listen! You don't run your rockets! On Earth you keep a motor going because when it stops, you do. But out here you have to use your motor to stop, but not to keep on going. Get it? When you do come out, don't burn your rockets more than half a second at a time."

The Chief's voice came booming:

"*Right, Joe! Here I come!*"

There was a billowing of frantically writhing fumes, which darted madly in every direction until they ceased to be. The Chief in his insect-like contraption came bolting out of the hole which was the airlock. He was a good half-mile away. The rocket fumes ceased. He kept on going. Joe heard him swear. The Chief felt the utterly helpless sensation of a man in a car when his brakes don't work. But a moment later the braking rockets did flare briefly, yet still too long. The Chief was not only stopped, but drifting backwards toward the Platform. He evidently tried to turn, and he spun as dizzily as Joe had done. But after a moment he stopped-- almost. There were, then, two red-painted things in space, somewhat like giant water-spiders floating forlornly in emptiness. They seemed very remote from the great bright steel Platform and that gigantic ball which was Earth, turning very slowly and filling a good fourth of all that could be seen.

"Suppose you head toward me, Chief," said Joe absorbedly. "Aim to pass, and remember that what you have to estimate is not where I am, but where you have to put on the brakes to stop close by. That's where you use your braking-rockets."

The Chief tried it. He came to a stop a quarter-mile past Joe.

"*I'm heavy-handed*," said his voice disgustedly.

"I'll try to join you," said Joe.

He did try. He stopped a little short. The two weird objects drifted almost to-gether. The Chief was upside down with regard to Joe. Presently he was sidewise on.

"This takes thinking," said Joe ruefully.

A voice in his headphones, from the Platform, said:

"*That rocket from Earth is still accelerating. Still at three gravities. It looks like it isn't defective. It might be carrying a man. Hadn't you better come in?*"

The Chief growled: "*We won't be any safer there! I want to get the hang of this.*" Then his voice changed sharply. "*Joe! D'you get that?*"

Joe heard his own voice, very cold.

"I didn't. I do now. Brown, I'd suggest a guided missile at that rocket coming up. If there's a man in it, he's coming up to take over guided missiles that'll overtake him, and try to smash the Platform by direct control, since proximity fuses don't work. I'd smash him as far away as possible."

Brown's voice came very curt and worried. "*Right.*"

There was an eruption of rocket fumes from the side of the Platform. Something went foaming away toward Earth. It dwindled with incredible rapidity. Then Joe said:

"Chief, I think we'd better go down and meet that rocket. We'll learn to handle these wagons on the way. I think we're going to have a fight on our hands. Whoever's in that rocket isn't coming up just to shake hands with us."

He steadied the small red vehicle and pointed it for Earth. He added:

"I'm firing a six-two solid-fuel job, Chief. Counting three. Three--two--one."

His mount vanished in rocket fumes. But after six seconds at two gravities acceleration the rocket burned out. The Chief had fired a matching rocket. They were miles apart, but speeding Earthward on very nearly identical courses.

The Platform grew smaller. That was their only proof of motion.

A very, very long time passed. The Chief fired his steering rockets to bring him closer to Joe. It did not work. He had to aim for Joe and fire a blast to move noticeably nearer. Presently he would have to blast again to keep from passing.

Joe made calculations in his head. He worried. He and the Chief were speeding Earthward--away from the Platform--at more than four miles a minute, but it was not enough. The manned rocket was accelerating at a great deal more than that rate. And if the Platform's enemies down on Earth had sent a manned rocket up to destroy the Platform, the man in it would have ways of defending himself. He would expect guided missiles--but he probably wouldn't expect to be attacked by space wagons.

Joe said suddenly:

"Chief! I'm going to burn a twelve-two. We've got to match velocities coming back. Join me? Three--two--one."

He fired a twelve-two. Twelve seconds burning, two gravities acceleration.

It built up his speed away from the Platform to a rate which would have been breathless, on Earth. But here there was no sensation of motion, and the distances were enormous. Things which happen in space happen with insensate violence and incredible swiftness. But long, long, long intervals elapse between events. The twelve-two rocket burned out. The Chief had matched that also.

Brown's voice in the headphones said, "*The rocket's cut acceleration. It's floating up, now. It should reach our orbit fifty miles behind us. But our missile should hit it in forty seconds.*"

"I wouldn't bet on that," said Joe coldly. "Figure interception data for the Chief and me. Make it fast!"

He spotted the Chief, a dozen miles away and burning his steering rockets to close, again. The Chief had the hang of it, now. He didn't try to steer. He drove toward Joe.

But nothing happened. And nothing happened. And nothing happened. The two tiny space wagons were 90 miles from the Platform, which was now merely a glittering speck, hardly brighter than the brightest stars.

There was a flare of light to Earthward. It was brighter than the sun. The light vanished.

Brown's voice came in the headphones, "*Our missile went off 200 miles short! He sent an interceptor to set it off!*"

"Then he's dangerous," said Joe. "There'll be war rockets coming up any second now for him to control from right at hand. We won't be fighting rockets controlled from 4,000 miles away! They've found proximity fuses don't work, so he's going to work in close. Give us our course and data, quick! The Chief and I have got to try to smash things!"

The two tiny space wagons--like stick-insects in form, absurdly painted a brilliant red--seemed inordinately lonely. It was hardly possible to pick out the Platform with the naked eyes. The Earth was thousands of miles below. Joe and the Chief, in space suits, rode tiny metal frameworks in an emptiness more vast, more lonely, more terrible than either could have imagined.

Then the war rockets started up. There were eight of them. They came out to do murder at ten gravities acceleration.

9

But even at ten gravities' drive it takes time to travel 4,000 miles. At three, and coasting a great deal of the way, it takes much longer. The Platform circled Earth in four hours and a little more. Anything intending interception and rising straight up needed to start skyward long before the Platform was overhead. A three-g rocket would start while the Platform was still below the western horizon from its launching-spot. Especially if it planned to coast part of its journey--and a three-gravity rocket would have to coast most of the way.

So there was time. Coasting, the rising manned rocket would be losing speed. If it planned to go no higher than the Platform's orbit, its upward velocity would be zero there. If it were intercepted 500 miles down, it would be rising at an almost leisurely rate, and Joe and the Chief could check their Earthward plunge and match its rising rate.

This they did. But what they couldn't do was match its orbital velocity, which was zero. They had the Platform's eastward speed to start with--over 200 miles a minute. No matter how desperately they fired braking-rockets, they couldn't stop and maneuver around the rising control-ship. Inevitably they would simply flash past it in the fraction of an instant. To fire their tiny guided missiles on ahead would be almost to assure that they would miss. Also, the enemy ship was manned. It could fight back.

But Joe had been on the receiving end of one attack in space. It wasn't much experience, but it was more than anybody but he and his own crew possessed.

"Chief," said Joe softly into his helmet-mike, as if by speaking softly he could keep from being overheard, "get close enough to me to see what I do, and do it too. I can't tell you more. Whoever's running this rocket might know English."

There was a flaring of vapor in space. The Chief was using his steering-rockets to draw near.

Joe spun his little space wagon about, so that it pointed back in the direction from which he had come. He had four guided missiles, demolition type. Very deliberately, he fired the four of them astern--away from the rising rocket. They were relatively low-speed missiles, intended to blow up a robot ship that couldn't be hooked onto, because it was traveling too much faster or slower than the Platform it was intended to reach. The missiles went away. Then Joe faced about again in the direction of his prospective target. The Chief fumed--Joe heard him--but he duplicated Joe's maneuver. He faced his own eccentric vessel in the direction of its line of flight.

Then his fuming suddenly ceased. Joe's headphones brought his explosive grunt when he suddenly saw the idea.

"Joe! I wish you could talk Indian! I could kiss you for this trick!"

Brown's voice said anxiously: *"I'm going to let that manned rocket have a couple more shots."*

"Let us get by first," said Joe. "Then maybe you can use them on the bombs coming up."

He could see the trails of war-rockets on the way out from Earth. They were infinitesimal threads of vapor. They were the thinnest possible filaments of gossamer white. But they enlarged as they rose. They were climbing at better than two miles per second, now, and still increasing their speed.

But the arena in which this conflict took place was so vast that everything seemed to take place in slow motion. There was time to reason out not only the method of attack from Earth, but the excuse for it. If the Platform vanished from space, no matter from what cause, its enemies would announce vociferously that it had been destroyed by its own atomic bombs, exploding spontaneously. Even in the face of proof of murder, enemy nations would stridently insist that bombs intended for the enslavement of humanity--in the Platform--had providentially detonated and removed that instrument of war-mongering scoundrelly imperialists from the skies. There might be somebody, somewhere, who would believe it.

Joe and the Chief were steadied now nearly on a line to intercept the rising manned rocket. They had already fired their missiles, which trailed them. They went into battle, not prepared to shoot, but with their ammunition expended. For which there was excellent reason.

Something came foaming toward them from the nearby man-carrying rocket. It seemed like a side-spout from the column of vapor rising from Earth. Actually it was a guided missile.

"Now we dodge," said Joe cheerfully. "Remember the trick of this maneuvering business!"

It was simple. Speeding toward the rising assassin, and with his missiles rushing toward them, the relative speeds of the wagons and the missiles were added together. If the space wagons dodged, the missile operator had less time to swing his guided rockets to match the change of target course. And besides, the attacker hadn't made a single turn in space. Not yet. He might know that a rocket doesn't go where it's pointed, as a matter of theory. He might even know intellectually that the final speed and course of a rocket is the sum of all its previous speeds and courses. But he hadn't used the knowledge Joe and the Chief had.

Something rushed at them. They went into evasive action. And they didn't merely turn the noses of their space wagons. They flung them about end-for-end, and blasted. They used wholly different accelerations at odd angles. Joe shot away from Earth on steering rocket thrust, and touched off a four-three while he faced toward Earth's north pole, and halfway along that four-second rush he flipped his craft in a somersault and the result was nearly a right-angled turn. When the four-three burned out he set off a twelve-two, and halfway through its burning fired a three-two with it, so that at the beginning he had two gravities acceleration, then four gravities for three seconds, and then two again.

With long practice, a man might learn marksmanship in space. But all a man's judgment of speeds is learned on Earth, where things always, always, always move steadily. Nobody making his first space-flight could possibly hit such targets as Joe and the Chief made of themselves. The man in the enemy rocket was making his first flight. Also, Joe and the Chief had an initial velocity of 200 miles a minute toward him. The marksman in the rising rocket hadn't a chance. He fired four more missiles and tried desperately to home them in. But----

They flashed past his rising course. And then they were quite safe from his fire, because it would take a very long time indeed for anything he shot after them to catch up. But their missiles had still to pass him--and Joe and the Chief could steer them without any concern about their own safety or anything else but a hit.

They made a hit.

Two of the eight little missiles flashed luridly, almost together, where the radar-pips showed the rocket to be. Then there were two parts to the rocket, separating. One was small and one was fairly large. Another demolition-missile hit the larger section. Still another exploded as that was going to pieces. The smaller fragment ceased to be important. The explosions weren't atomic bombs, of course. They were only demolition-charges. But they demolished the manned rocket admirably.

Brown's voice came in the headphones, still tense. "*You got it! How about the others?*"

Joe felt a remarkable exhilaration. Later he might think about the poor devil-- there could have been only one--who had been destroyed some 3,700 miles above the surface of the Earth. He might think unhappily of that man as a victim of hatred rather than as a hater. He might become extremely uncomfortable about this, but at the moment he felt merely that he and the Chief had won a startling victory.

"I think," he said, "that you can treat them with silent contempt. They won't have proximity fuses. Those friends of ours who want so badly to kill us have found that proximity fuses don't work. Unless one is on a collision course I don't think you need to do anything about them."

The Chief was muttering to himself in Mohawk, twenty miles away. Joe said: "Chief, how about getting back to the Platform?"

The Chief growled. "*My great-grandfather would disown me! Winning a fight and no scalp to show! Not even counting coup! He'd disown me!*"

But Joe saw his rockets flare, away off against the stars.

The war rockets were very near, now. They still emitted monstrous jettings of thick white vapor. They climbed up with incredible speed. One went by Joe at a distance of little more than a mile, and its fumes eddied out to half that before they thinned to nothingness. They went on and on and on....

They burned out somewhere. It would be a long time before they fell back to Earth. Hours, probably. Then they would be meteors. They'd vaporize before they touched solidity. They wouldn't even explode.

But Joe and the Chief rode back to the Platform. It was surprising how hard it was to match speed with it again, to make a good entrance into the giant lock. They barely made it before the Platform made its plunge into that horrible blackness which was the Earth's shadow. And Joe was very glad they did make it before then. He wouldn't have liked to be merely astride a skinny framework in that ghastly darkness, with the monstrous blackness of the Abyss seeming to be trying to devour him.

Haney met them in the airlock. He grinned.

"Nice job, Joe! Nice job, Chief!" he said warmly. "Uh--the Lieutenant Commander wants you to report to him, Joe. Right away."

Joe cocked an eyebrow at him.

"What for?"

Haney spread out his hands. The Chief grunted. "That guy bothers me. I'll bet, Joe, he's going to explain you shouldn't've gone out when he didn't want you to. Me, I'm keeping away from him!"

The Chief shed his space suit and swaggered away, as well as anyone could swagger while walking on what happened to be the ceiling, from Joe's point of view. Joe put his space gear in its proper place. He went to the small cubbyhole that Brown had appropriated for the office of the Platform Commander. Joe went in, naturally without saluting.

Brown sat in a fastened-down chair with thigh grips holding him in place. He was writing. On Joe's entry, he carefully put the pen down on a magnetized plate that would hold it until he wanted it again. Otherwise it could have floated anywhere about the room.

"Mr. Kenmore," said Brown awkwardly, "you did a very nice piece of work. It's too bad you aren't in the Navy."

Joe said: "It did work out pretty fortunately. It's lucky the Chief and I were out practicing, but now we can take off when a rocket's reported, any time."

Brown cleared his throat. "I can thank you personally," he said unhappily, "and I do. But--really this situation is intolerable! How can I report this affair? I can't suggest commendation, or a promotion, or--anything! I don't even know how to refer to you! I am going to ask you, Mr. Kenmore, to put through a request that your status be clarified. I would imagine that your status would mean a rank--hm--about equivalent to a lieutenant junior grade in the Navy."

Joe grinned.

"I have--ah--prepared a draft you might find helpful," said Brown earnestly. "It's necessary for something to be done. It's urgent! It's important!"

"Sorry," said Joe. "The important thing to me is getting ready to load up the Platform with supplies from Earth. Excuse me."

He went out of the office. He made his way to the quarters assigned himself and his crew. Mike greeted him with reproachful eyes. Joe waved his hand.

"Don't say it, Mike! The answer is yes. See that the tanks are refilled, and new rockets put in place. Then you and Haney go out and practice. But no farther than ten miles from the Platform. Understand?"

"No!" said Mike rebelliously. "It's a dirty trick!"

"Which," Joe assured him, "I commit only because there's a robot ship from Bootstrap coming up any time now. And we'll need to pick it up and tow it here."

He went to the control-room to see if he could get a vision connection to Earth.

He got the beam, and he got Sally on the screen. A report of the attack on the Platform had evidently already gone down to Earth. Sally's expression was somehow drawn and haunted. But she tried to talk lightly.

"Derring-do and stuff, Joe?" she asked. "How does it feel to be a victorious warrior?"

"It feels rotten," he told her. "There must have been somebody in the rocket we blew up. He felt like a patriot, I guess, trying to murder us; But I feel like a butcher."

"Maybe you didn't do it," she said. "Maybe the Chief's bombs----"

"Maybe," said Joe. He hesitated. "Hold up your hand."

She held it up. His ring was still on it. She nodded. "Still there. When will you be back?"

He shook his head. He didn't know. It was curious that one wanted so badly to talk to a girl after doing something that was blood-stirring--and left one rather sickish afterward. This business of space travel and even space battle was what he'd dreamed of, and he still wanted it. But it was very comforting to talk to Sally, who hadn't had to go through any of it.

"Write me a letter, will you?" he asked. "We can't tie up this beam very long."

"I'll write you all the news that's allowed to go out," she assured him. "Be seeing you, Joe."

Her image faded from the screen. And, thinking it over, he couldn't see that either of them had said anything of any importance at all. But he was very glad they'd talked together.

The first robot ship came up some eight hours later--two revolutions after the television call. Mike was ready hours in advance, fidgeting. The robot ship started up while the Platform was over the middle of the Pacific. It didn't try to make a spiral approach as all other ships had done. It came straight up, and it started from the ground. No pushpots. Its take-off rockets were monsters. They pushed upward at ten gravities until it was out of atmosphere, and then they stepped up to fifteen. Much later, the robot turned on its side and fired orbital speed rockets to match velocity with the Platform.

There were two reasons for the vertical rise, and the high acceleration. If a robot ship went straight up, it wouldn't pass over enemy territory until it was high enough to be protected by the Platform. And--it costs fuel to carry fuel to be burned. So if the rocketship could get up speed for coasting to orbit in the first couple of hundred miles, it needn't haul its fuel so far. It was economical to burn one's fuel fast and get an acceleration that would kill a human crew. Hence robots.

The landing of the first robot ship at the Platform was almost as matter-of-fact as if it had been done a thousand times before. From the Platform its dramatic take-off couldn't be seen, of course. It first appeared aloft as a pip on a radar screen. Then Mike prepared to go out and hook on to it and tow it in. He was in his space suit and in the landing lock, though his helmet faceplate was still open. A loudspeaker boomed suddenly in Brown's voice: "*Evacuate airlock and prepare to take off!*"

Joe roared: "Hold that!"

Brown's voice, very official, came: "*Withhold execution of that order. You should not be in the airlock, Mr. Kenmore. You will please make way for operational procedure.*"

"We're checking the space wagon," snapped Joe. "That's operational procedure!"

The loudspeaker said severely: "*The checking should have been done earlier!*"

There was silence. Mike and Joe, together, painstakingly checked over the very many items that had to be made sure. Every rocket had to have its firing circuit inspected. The tanks' contents and pressure verified. The air connection to Mike's space suit. The air pressure. The device that made sure that air going to Mike's space suit was neither as hot as metal in burning sunlight, nor cold as the chill of a shadow in space.

Everything checked. Mike straddled his red-painted mount. Joe left the lock and said curtly:

"Okay to pump the airlock. Okay to open airlock doors when ready. Go ahead."

Mike went out, and Joe watched from a port in the Platform's hull. The drone from Earth was five miles behind the Platform in its orbit, and twenty miles below, and all of ten miles off-course. Joe saw Mike scoot the red space wagon to it, stop short with a sort of cocky self-assurance, hook on to the tow-ring in the floating space-barge's nose, and blast off back toward the Platform with it in tow.

Mike had to turn about and blast again to check his motion when he arrived. And then he and Haney--Haney in the other space wagon--nudged at it and tugged at it and got it in the great spacelock. They went in after it and the lock doors closed.

Neither Mike nor Haney were out of their space suits when Kent brought Joe a note. A note was an absurdity in the Platform. But this was a formal communication from Brown.

"From: Lt. Comdr. Brown

To: Mr. Kenmore

Subject: Cooperation and courtesy in rocket recovery vehicle launchings.

1. There is a regrettable lack of coordination and courtesy in the launching of rocket-recovery vehicles (space wagons) in the normal operation of the Platform.

2. The maintenance of discipline and efficiency requires that the commanding officer maintain overall control of all operations at all times.

3. Hereafter when a space vehicle of any type is to be launched, the

commanding officer will be notified in writing not less than one hour before such launching.

4. The time of such proposed launching will be given in such notification in hours and minutes and seconds, Greenwich Mean Time.

5. All commands for launching will be given by the commanding officer or an officer designated by him."

Joe received the memo as he was in the act of writing a painstaking report on the maneuver Mike had carried out. Mike was radiant as he discussed possible improvements with later and better equipment. After all, this had been a lucky landing. For a robot to end up no more than 30 miles from its target, after a journey of 4,000 miles, and with a difference in velocity that was almost immeasurable--such good fortune couldn't be expected as a regular thing. The space wagons were tiny. If they had to travel long distances to recover erratic ships coming up from Earth----

Joe forgot all about Lieutenant Commander Brown and his memo when the mail was distributed. Joe had three letters from Sally. He read them in the great living compartment of the Platform with its sixty-foot length and its carpet on floor and ceiling, and the galleries without stairs outside the sleeping cabins. He sat in a chair with thigh grips to hold him in place, and he wore a gravity simulation harness. It was necessary. The regular crew of the Platform, by this time, couldn't have handled space wagons in action against enemy manned rockets. Joe meant to stay able to take acceleration.

It was just as he finished his mail that Brent came in.

"Big news!" said Brent. "They're building a big new ship of new design--almost half as big as the Platform. With concreted metal they can do it in weeks."

"What's it for?" demanded Joe.

"It'll be a human base on the Moon," said Brent relievedly. "An expedition will start in six weeks, according to plan. As long as we're the only American base in space, we're going to be shot at. But a base on the Moon will be invulnerable. So they're going ahead with it."

Joe said hopefully:

"Any orders for me to join it?"

Brent shook his head. "We're to be loaded up with supplies for the Moon expedition. We're to be ready to take a robot ship every round. Actually, they can't hope to send us more than two a day for a while, but even that'll be eighty tons of supplies to be stored away."

The Chief grumbled, but somehow his grumbling did not sound genuine. "They're going to the Moon--and leave us here to do stevedore stuff?" His tone was odd. He looked at a letter he'd been reading and gave up pretense. He said self-consciously: "Listen, you guys.... My tribe's got all excited. I just got a letter from the council. They've been having an argument about me. Wanna hear?"

He was a little amused, and a little embarrassed, but something had happened to make him feel good.

"Let's have it," said Joe. Mike was very still in another chair. He didn't look up, though he must have heard. Haney cocked an interested ear.

The Chief said awkwardly, "You know--us Mohawks are kinda proud. We got something to be proud of. We were one of the Five Nations, when that was a sort of United Nations and all Europe was dog-eat-dog. My tribe had a big pow-wow about me. There's a tribe member that's a professor of anthropology out in Chicago. He was there. And a couple of guys that do electronic research, and doctors and farmers and all sorts of guys. All Mohawks. They got together in tribal council."

He stopped and flushed under his dark skin. "I wouldn't tell you, only you guys are in on it."

Still he hesitated. Joe found a curious picture forming in his mind. He'd known the Chief a long time, and he knew that part of the tribe lived in Brooklyn, and individual members were widely scattered. But still there was a certain remote village which to all the tribesmen was home. Everybody went back there from time to time, to rest from the strangeness of being Indians in a world of pale-skinned folk.

Joe could almost imagine the council. There'd be old, old men who could nearly remember the days of the tribe's former glory, who'd heard stories of forest warfare and zestful hunts, and scalpings and heroic deeds from their grandfathers. But there were also doctors and lawyers and technical men in that council which met to talk about the Chief.

"It's addressed to me," said the Chief with sudden clumsiness, "in the World-by-itself Canoe. That's the Platform here. And it says--I'll have to translate, because it's in Mohawk." He took a deep breath. "It says, 'We your tribesmen have heard of your journeyings off the Earth where men have never traveled before. This has given us great pride, that one of our tribe and kin had ventured so valiantly.'" The Chief grinned abashedly. He went on. "'In full assembly, the elders of the tribe have held counsel on a way to express their pride in you, and in the friends you have made who accompanied you. It was proposed that you be given a new name to be borne by your sons after you. It was proposed that the tribe accept from each of its members a gift to be given you in the name of the tribe. But these were not considered great enough. Therefore the tribe, in full council, has decreed that your name shall be named at every tribal council of the Mohawks from this day to the end of time, as one the young braves would do well to copy in all ways. And the names of your friends Joe Kenmore, Mike Scandia, and Thomas Haney shall also be named as friends whose like all young braves should strive to seek out and to be.'"

The Chief sweated a little, but he looked enormously proud. Joe went over to him and shook hands warmly. The Chief almost broke his fingers. It was, of course, as high an honor as could be paid to anybody by the people who paid it.

Haney said awkwardly, "Lucky they don't know me like you do, Chief. But it's swell!"

Which it was. But Mike hadn't said a word. The Chief said exuberantly:

"Did you hear that, Mike? Every Mohawk for ten thousand years is gonna be told that you were a swell guy! Crazy, huh?"

Mike said in an odd voice: "Yeah. I didn't mean that, Chief. It's fine! But I--I got a letter. I--never thought to get a letter like this."

He looked unbelievingly at the paper in his hands.

"Mash note?" asked the Chief. His tone was a little bit harsh. Mike was a midget. And there were women who were fools. It would be unbearable if some half-witted female had written Mike the sort of gushing letter that some half-witted females might write.

Mike shook his head, with an odd, quick smile.

"Not what you think, Chief. But it is from a girl. She sent me her picture. It's a--swell letter. I'm--going to answer it. You can look at her picture. She looks kind of--nice."

He handed the Chief a snapshot. The Chief's face changed. Haney looked over his shoulder. He passed the picture to Joe and said ferociously: "You Mike! You dog-goned Don Juan! The Chief and me have got to warn her what kinda guy you are! Stealing from blind men! Fighting cops----"

Joe looked at the picture. It was a very sweet small face, and the eyes that looked out of the photograph were very honest and yearning. And Joe understood. He grinned at Mike. Because this girl had the distinctive look that Mike had. She was a midget, too.

"She's--thirty-nine inches tall," said Mike, almost stunned. "She's just two inches shorter than me. And--she says she doesn't mind being a midget so much since she heard about me. I'm going to write her."

But it would be, of course, a long time before there was a way for mail to get down to Earth.

It was a long time. Now it was possible to send up robot rockets to the Platform. They came up. When the second arrived, Haney went out to pull it in. Joe forgot to notify Brown, in writing, an hour before launching a rocket recovery vehicle (space wagon) according to paragraph 3 of the formal memo, nor the time of launching in hours, minutes, etc., by Greenwich Mean Time (paragraph 4), nor was the testing of all equipment made before moving it into the airlock. This was because the testing equipment was in the airlock, where it belonged. And the commands for launching were not given by Brown or an officer designated by him, because Joe forgot all about it.

Brown made a stormy scene about the matter, and Joe was honestly apologetic, but the Chief and Haney and Mike glared venomously.

The result was completely inconclusive. Joe had not been put under Brown's command. He and his crew were the only people on the Platform physically in shape to operate the space wagons, considering the acceleration involved. Brent and the others were wearing gravity simulators, and were building back to strength. But they weren't up to par as yet. They'd been in space too long.

So there was nothing Brown could do. He retreated into icily correct, outraged dignity. And the others hauled in and unloaded rockets as they arrived. They came up fast. The processes of making them had been improved. They could be made faster, heated to sintering temperature faster, and the hulls cooled to usefulness in a quarter of the former time. The production of space ship hulls went up to four a day, while the molds for the Moonship were being worked even faster. The Moonship, actually, was assembled from precast individual cells which then were welded together. It would have features the Platform lacked, because it was designed to be a base for exploration and military activities in addition to research.

But only twenty days after the recovery and docking of the first robot ship to rise, a new sort of ship entirely came blindly up as a robot. The little space wagons hauled it to the airlock and inside. They unloaded it--and it was no longer a robot. It was a modified hull designed for the duties of a tug in space. It could carry a crew of four, and its cargohold was accessible from the cabin. It had an airlock. More, it carried a cargo of solid-fuel rockets which could be shifted to firing racks outside its hull. Starting from the platform, where it had no effective weight, it was capable of direct descent to the Earth without spiralling or atmospheric braking. To make that descent it would, obviously, expend four-fifths of its loaded weight in rockets. And since it had no weight at the Platform, but only mass, it was capable of far-ranging journeying. It could literally take off from the Platform and reach the Moon and land on it, and then return to the Platform.

But that had to wait.

"Sure we could do it," agreed Joe, when Mike wistfully pointed out the possibility. "It would be good to try it. But unfortunately, space exploration isn't a stunt. We've gotten this far because--somebody wanted to do something. But----" Then he said, "It could be done and the United Nations wouldn't do it. So the United States had to, or--somebody else would have. You can figure who that would be, and what use they'd make of space travel! So it's important. It's more important than stunt flights we could make!"

"Nobody could stop us if we wanted to take off!" Mike said rebelliously.

"True," Joe said. "But we four can stand three gravities acceleration and handle any more manned rockets that start out here. We've lived through plenty more than that! But Brent and the others couldn't put up a fight in space. They're wearing harness now, and they're coming back to strength. But we're going to stay right here and do stevedoring--and fighting too, if it comes to that--until the job is done."

And that was the way it was, too. Of stevedoring there was plenty. Two robot ships a day for weeks on end. Three ships a day for a time. Four. Sometimes things went smoothly, and the little space wagons could go out and bring back the great, rocket-scarred hulls from Earth. But once in three times the robots were going too fast or too slow. The space wagons couldn't handle them. Then the new ship, the space tug, went out and hooked onto the robot with a chain and used the power it had to bring them to their destination. And sometimes the robots didn't climb straight. At least once the space tug captured an erratic robot 400 miles from its destination and hauled it in. It used some heavy solid-fuel rockets on that trip.

The Platform had become, in fact, a port in space, though so far it had had only arrivals and no departures. Its storage compartments almost bulged with fuel stores and food stores and equipment of every imaginable variety. It had a stock of rockets which were enough to land it safely on Earth, though there was surely no intention of doing so. It had food and air for centuries. It had repair parts for all its own equipment. And it had weapons. It contained, in robot hulls anchored to its sides, enough fissionable material to conduct a deadly war--which was only stored for transfer to the Moon base when that should be established.

And it had communication with Earth of high quality. So far the actual mail was only a one-way service, but even entertainment came up, and news. Once there was a television shot of the interior of the Shed. It was carefully scrambled before transmission, but it was a heartening sight. The Shed on the TV screen appeared a place of swarming activity. Robot hulls were being made. They were even improved, fined down to ten tons of empty weight apiece, and their controls were assembly line products now. And there was the space flight simulator with men practicing in it, although for the time being only robots were taking off from Earth. And there was the Moonship.

It didn't look like the Platform, but rather like something a child might have put together out of building blocks. It was built up out of welded-together cells with strengthening members added. It was 60 feet high from the floor and twice as long, and it did not weigh nearly what it seemed to. Already it was being clad in that thick layer of heat insulation it would need to endure the two-week-long lunar night. It could take off very soon now.

The pictured preparations back on Earth meant round-the-clock drudgery for Joe and the others. They wore themselves out. But the storage space on the Platform filled up. Days and weeks went by. Then there came a time when literally nothing else could be stored, so Joe and his crew made ready to go back to Earth.

They ate hugely and packed a very small cargo in their ship. They picked up one bag of mail and four bags of scientific records and photographs which had only been transmitted by facsimile TV before. They got into the space tug. It floated free.

"*You will fire in ten seconds*," said a crisp voice in Joe's headphones. "*Ten ... nine ... eight ... seven ... six ... five ... four ... three ... two ... one ... fire!*"

Joe crooked his index finger. There was an explosive jolt. Rockets flamed terribly in emptiness. The space tug rushed toward the west. The Platform seemed to dwindle with startling suddenness. It seemed to rush away and become lost in the myriads of stars. The space tug accelerated at four gravities in the direction opposed to its orbital motion.

As the acceleration built up, it dropped toward Earth and home like a tumbled stone.

10

There was bright sunshine at the Shed, not a single cloud in all the sky. The radar bowls atop the roof--they seemed almost invisibly small compared with its vastness--wavered and shifted and quivered. Completely invisible beams of microwaves lanced upward. Atop the Shed, in the communication room, there was the busy quiet of absolute intentness. Signals came down and were translated into visible records which fed instantly into computers. Then the computers clicked and hummed and performed incomprehensible integrations, and out of their slot-mouths poured billowing ribbons of printed tape. Men read those tapes and talked crisply into microphones, and their words went swiftly aloft again.

Down by the open eastern door of the Shed at the desert's edge, Sally Holt and Joe's father waited together, watching the sky. Sally was white and scared. Joe's father patted her shoulder reassuringly.

"He'll make it, all right," said Sally, dry-throated.

Joe's father nodded. "Of course he will!" But his voice was not steady.

"Nothing could happen to him now!" said Sally fiercely.

"Of course not," said Joe's father.

A loudspeaker close to them said abruptly: "*Nineteen miles.*"

There was a tiny, straggling thread of white visible in the now. It thinned out to nothingness, but its nearest part flared out and flared out and flared out. It grew larger, came closer with a terrifying speed.

"*Twelve miles*," said the speaker harshly. "*Rockets firing.*"

The downward-hurtling trail of smoke was like a crippled plane falling flaming from the sky, except that no plane ever fell so fast.

At seven miles the white-hot glare of the rocket flames was visible even in broad daylight. At three miles the light was unbearably bright. At two, the light winked out. Sally saw something which glittered come plummeting toward the ground, unsupported.

It fell almost half a mile before rocket fumes flung furiously out again. Then it checked. Visibly, its descent was slowed. It dropped more slowly, and more slowly, and more slowly still....

It hung in mid-air a quarter-mile up. Then there was a fresh burst of rocket fumes, more monstrous than ever, and it went steadily downward, touched the ground, and stayed there spurting terrible incandescent flames for seconds. Then the bottom flame went out. An instant later there were no more flames at all.

Sally began to run toward the ship. She stopped. A procession of rumbling, clanking, earth-moving machinery moved out of the Shed and toward the upright space tug. Prosaically, a bulldozer lowered its wide blade some fifty yards from the ship. It pushed a huge mass of earth before it, covering over the scorched and impossibly hot sand about the rocket's landing place. Other bulldozers began to circle methodically around and around, overturning the earth and burying the hot surface stuff. Water trucks sprayed, and thin steam arose.

But also an exit-port opened and Joe stood in the opening.

Then Sally began to run again.

* * * * *

Joe sat at dinner in the major's quarters. Major Holt was there, and Joe's father, and Sally.

"It feels good," said Joe warmly, "to use a knife and fork again, and to pick food up from a plate where it stays until it's picked up!"

"The crew of the Platform----" Major Holt began.

"They're all right," said Joe, with his mouth full. "They're wearing gravity simulator harness. Brent's got his up to three-quarters gravity. They get tired, wearing the harness. They sleep better. Everything's fine! They can handle the space wagons we left and they've got guided missiles to spare! They're all right!"

Joe's father said unsteadily, "You'll stay on Earth a while now, son?"

Sally moved quickly. She looked up, tense. But Joe said, "They're going to get the Moonship up, sir. We came back--my gang and me--to help train the crew. We only have a week to do it in, but we've got some combat tactics to show them on the training gadget in the Shed." He added anxiously, "And, sir--they'll have to take the Moonship off in a spiral orbit. She can't go straight up! That means she's got to pass over enemy territory, and--we've got to have a real escort for her. A fighting escort. It's planned for the space tug to take off a few minutes after the Moonship and blast along underneath. We'll dump guided missiles out--like drones--and if anything comes along we can start their rockets and fight our way through. And we four have had more experience than anybody else. We're needed!"

"You've done enough, surely!" Sally cried.

"The United States," said Joe awkwardly, "is going to take over the Moon. I--can't miss having a hand in that! Not if it's at all possible!"

"I'm afraid you will miss it, Joe," Major Holt said detachedly. "The occupation of the Moon will be a Navy enterprise. Space Exploration Project facilities are being used to prepare for it, but the Navy won the latest battle of the Pentagon. The Navy takes over the Moon."

Joe looked startled. "But----"

"You're Space Exploration personnel," said the major with the same coolness. "You will be used to instruct naval personnel, and your space tug will be asked to go along to the Platform as an auxiliary vessel. For purposes of assisting in the landing of the Moonship at the Platform, you understand. You'll haul her away from the Platform when she's refueled and supplied, so she can start off for the Moon. But the occupation of the Moon will be strictly Navy."

Joe's expression became carefully unreadable. "I think," he said evenly, "I'd better not comment."

Major Holt nodded. "Very wise--not that we'd repeat anything you did say. But the point is, Joe, that just one day before the Moonship does take off, the United Nations will be informed that it is a United States naval vessel. The doctrine of the freedom of space--like the freedom of the seas--will be promulgated. And the United States will say that a United States naval task force is starting off into space on an official mission. To attack a Space Exploration ship is one thing. That's like a scientific expedition. But to fire on an American warship on official business is a declaration of war. Especially since that ship can shoot back--and will."

Joe listened. He said, "It's daring somebody to try another Pearl Harbor?"

"Exactly," said the major. "It's time for us to be firm--now that we can back it up. I don't think the Moonship will be fired on."

"But they'll need me and my gang just the same," said Joe slowly, "for tugboat work at the Platform?"

"Exactly," said the major.

"Then," Joe said doggedly, "they get us. My gang will gripe about being edged out of the trip. They won't like it. But they'd like backing out still less. We'll play it the way it's dealt--but we won't pretend to like it."

Major Holt's expression did not change at all, but Joe had an odd feeling that the major approved of him.

"Yes. That's right, Joe," his father added. "You--you'll have to go aloft once more, son. After that, we'll talk it over."

Sally hadn't said a word during the discussion, but she'd watched Joe every second. Later, out on the porch of the major's quarters, she had a great deal to say. But that couldn't affect the facts.

The world at large, of course, received no inkling of the events in preparation. The Shed and the town of Bootstrap and all the desert for a hundred-mile circle round about, were absolutely barred to all visitors. Anybody who came into that circle stayed in. Most people were kept out. All that anyone outside could discover was that enormous quantities of cryptic material had poured and still were pouring into the Shed. But this time security was genuinely tight. Educated guesses could be made, and they were made; but nobody outside the closed-in area save a very few top-ranking officials had any real knowledge. The world only knew that something drastic and remarkable was in prospect.

Mike, though, was able to write a letter to the girl who'd written him. Major Holt arranged it. Mike wrote his letter on paper supplied by Security, with ink supplied by Security, and while watched by Security officers. His letter was censored by Major Holt himself, and it did not reveal that Mike was back on Earth. But it did invite a reply--and Mike sweated as he waited for one.

The others had plenty to sweat about. Joe and Haney and the Chief were acting as instructors to the Moonship's crew. They taught practical space navigation. At first they thought they hadn't much to pass on, but they found out otherwise. They had to pass on data on everything from how to walk to how to drink coffee, how to eat, sleep, why one should wear gravity harness, and the manners and customs of ships in space. They had to show why in space fighting a ship might send missiles on before it, but would really expect to do damage with those it left behind. They had to warn of the dangers of unshielded sunshine, and the equal danger of standing in shadow for more than five minutes, and----

They had material for six months of instruction courses, but there was barely a week to pass it on. Joe was run ragged, but in spite of everything he managed to talk at some length with Sally. He found himself curiously anxious to discuss any number of things with his father, too, who suddenly appeared to be much more intelligent than Joe had ever noticed before.

He was almost unhappy when it was certain that the Moonship would take off for space on the following day. He talked about it with Sally the night before take-off.

"Look," he said awkwardly. "As far as I'm concerned this has turned out a pretty sickly business. But when we have got a base on the Moon, it'll be a good job done. There will be one thing that nobody can stop! Everybody's been living in terror of war. If we hold the Moon the cold war will be ended. You can't kick on my wanting to help end that!"

Sally smiled at him in the moonlight.

"And--meanwhile," said Joe clumsily, "well--when I come back we can do some serious talking about--well--careers and such things. Until then--no use. Right?"

Sally's smile wavered. "Very sensible," she agreed wrily. "And awfully silly, Joe. I know what kind of a career I want! What other fascinating topic do you know to talk about, Joe?"

"I don't know of any. Oh, yes! Mike got a letter from his girl. I don't know what she said, but he's walking on air."

"But it isn't funny!" said Sally indignantly. "Mike's a person! A fine person! If he'll let me, I'll write to his girl myself and--try to make friends with her so when you come back I--maybe I can be a sort of match-maker."

"That, I like!" Joe said warmly. "You're swell sometimes, Sally!"

Sally looked at him enigmatically in the moonlight.

"There are times when it seems to escape your attention," she observed.

*   *   *   *   *

The next morning she cried a little when he left her, to climb in the space tug which was so small a part of today's activity. Joe and his crew were the only living men who had ever made a round trip to the Platform and back. But now there was the Moonship to go farther than they'd been allowed. It was even clumsier in design than the Platform, though it was smaller. But it wasn't designed to stay in space. It was to rest on the powdery floor of a ring-mountain's central plain.

Let it get off into space, and somehow get to the Platform to reload. Then let it replace the rockets it would burn in this take-off and it could go on out to emptiness. It would make history as the first serious attempt by human beings to reach the Moon.

Joe and his followers would go along simply to handle guided missiles if it came to a fight, and to tow the Moonship to its wharf--the Platform--and out into midstream again when it resumed its journey. And that was all.

The Moonship lifted from the floor of the Shed to the sound of hundreds of pushpot engines.

Then the space tug roared skyward. Her take-off rockets here substituted for the pushpots. Her second-stage rockets were also of the nonpoisonous variety, because she fired them at a bare 60,000 feet. They were substitutes for the jatos the pushpots carried.

She was out in space when the third-stage rockets roared dully outside her hull.

When the Moonship crossed the west coast of Africa, the space tug was 400 miles below and 500 miles behind. When the Moonship crossed Arabia, the difference was 200 miles vertically and less than 100 in line.

Then the Moonship released small objects, steadied by gyroscopes and flung away by puffs of compressed air. The small objects spread out. Haney and Mike and the Chief had reloaded the firing racks from inside the ship, and now were intent upon control boards and radar. They pressed buttons. One by one, little puffs of smoke appeared in space. They had armed the little space missiles, setting off tiny flares which had no function except to prove that each missile was ready for use.

By the time the two space craft floated toward India, above an area from which war rockets had been known to rise, there were more little weapons floating with them. One screen of missiles hurtled on before the space tug, and another behind. Anything that came up from Earth would instantly be attacked by dozens of midget ships bent upon suicide.

Radar probed the space formation, but enemies of the fleet and the Platform very wisely did no more than probe. The Moonship and its attendants went across the Pacific, still rising. Above the longitude of Washington, the space tug left its former post and climbed, nudging the Moonship this way and that. And from behind, the Platform came floating splendidly.

Tiny figures in space suits extended the incredibly straight lines which were plastic hoses filled with air. Very, very gently indeed, the great, bulbous Platform and the squat, flat Moonship came together and touched. They moored in contact.

And then the inert small missiles that had floated below, all the way up, flared simultaneously. Their rockets emitted smoke. In fine alignment, they plunged forward through emptiness, swerved with a remarkable precision, and headed out for emptiness beyond the Platform's orbit. Their function had been to protect the Moonship on its way out. That function was performed. There were too many of them to recover, so they went out toward the stars.

When their rockets burned out they vanished. But a good hour later, when it was considered that they were as far out as they were likely to go, they began to blow up. Specks of flame, like the tiniest of new stars, flickered against the background of space.

But Joe and the others were in the Platform by then. They'd brought up mail for the crew. And they were back on duty.

The Platform seemed strange with the Moonship's crew aboard. It had been a gigantic artificial world with very few inhabitants. With twenty-five naval ratings about, plus the four of its regular crew, plus the space tug's complement, it seemed excessively crowded.

And it was busy. There were twenty-five new men to be guided as they applied what they'd been taught aground about life in space. It was three full Earthdays before the stores intended for the journey to the Moon and the maintenance of a base there really began to move. The tug and the space wagons had to be moored outside and reached only by space suits through small personnel airlocks.

And there was the matter of discipline. Lieutenant Commander Brown had been put in command of the Platform for experience in space. He was considered to be prepared for command of the Moonship by that experience. So now he turned over command of the Platform to Brent--he made a neat ceremony of it--and took over the ship that would go out to the Moon. He made another ceremony out of that.

In command of the Moonship, his manner to Joe was absolutely correct. He followed regulations to the letter--to a degree that left Joe blankly uncomprehending. But he wouldn't have gotten along in the Navy if he hadn't. He'd tried to do the same thing in the Platform, and it wasn't practical. But he ignored all differences between Joe and himself. He made no overtures of friendship, but that was natural. Unintentionally, Joe had defied him. He now deliberately overlooked all that, and Joe approved of him--within limits.

But Mike and Haney and the Chief did not. They laid for him. And they considered that they got him. When he took over the Moonship, Lieutenant Commander Brown naturally maintained naval discipline and required snappy, official naval salutes on all suitable occasions, even in the Platform. And Joe's gang privately tipped off the noncommissioned personnel of the Moonship. Thereafter, no enlisted man ever saluted Lieutenant Brown without first gently detaching his magnet-soled shoes from the floor. When a man was free, a really snappy salute gave a diverting result. The man's body tilted forward to meet his rising arm, the upward impetus was one-sided, and every man who saluted Brown immediately made a spectacular kowtow which left him rigidly at salute floating somewhere overhead with his back to Lieutenant Brown. With a little practice, it was possible to add a somersault to the other features. On one historic occasion, Brown walked clanking into a storeroom where a dozen men were preparing supplies for transfer to the Moonship. A voice cried, "Shun!" And instantly twelve men went floating splendidly about the storeroom, turning leisurely somersaults, all rigidly at salute, and all wearing regulation poker faces.

An order abolishing salutes in weightlessness followed shortly after.

It took four days to get the transfer of supplies properly started. It took eight to finish the job. Affixing fresh rockets to the outside of the Moonship's hull alone called for long hours in space suits. During this time Mike floated nearby in a space wagon. One of the Navy men was a trifle overcourageous. He affected to despise safety lines. Completing the hook-on of a landing rocket, he straightened up too abruptly and went floating off toward the Milky Way.

Mike brought him back. After that there was less trouble.

Even so, the Moonship and the Platform were linked together for thirteen full days, during which the Platform seemed extraordinarily crowded. On the fourteenth day the two ships sealed off and separated. Joe and his crew in the space tug hauled the Moonship a good five miles from the Platform.

The space tug returned to the Platform. A blinker signal came across the five-mile interval. It was a very crisp, formal, Navy-like message.

Then the newly-affixed rockets on the Moonship's hull spurted their fumes. The big ship began to move. Not outward from Earth, of course. That was where it was going. But it had the Platform's 12,000 miles per hour of orbital speed. If the bonds of gravitation could have been snapped at just the proper instant, that speed alone would have carried the Moonship all the way to its destination. But they couldn't. So the Moonship blasted to increase its orbital speed. It would swing out and out, and as the Earth's pull grew weaker with distance the same weight of rockets would move the same mass farther and farther toward the Moon. The Moonship's course would be a sort of slowly flattening curve, receding from Earth and becoming almost a straight line where Earth's and the Moon's gravitational fields cancelled each other.

From there, the Moonship would have only to brake its fall against a gravity one-sixth that of Earth, and reaching out a vastly shorter distance.

Joe and the others watched the roiling masses of rocket fumes as the ship seemed to grow infinitely small.

"We should've been in that ship," said Haney heavily when the naked eye could no longer pick it out. "We could've beat her to the Moon!"

Joe said nothing. He ached a little inside. But he reflected that the men who'd guided the Platform to its orbit had been overshadowed by himself and Haney and the Chief and Mike. A later achievement always makes an earlier one look small. Now the four of them would be forgotten. History would remember the commander of the Moonship.

Forgotten? Yes, perhaps. But the names of the four of them, Joe and Haney and the Chief and Mike, would still be remembered in a language Joe couldn't speak, in a small village he couldn't name, on those occasions when the Mohawk tribe met in formal council.

The Chief grumbled. Mike stared out the port with bitter envy.

"It was a dirty trick," growled the Chief. "We shoulda been part of the first gang ever to land on the Moon!"

Joe grimaced. His crew needed to be cured of feeling the same way he did.

"I wouldn't say this outside of our gang," said Joe carefully, "but if it hadn't been for us four that ship wouldn't be on the way at all. Haney figured the trick that got us back to Earth the first time, or else we'd have been killed. If we had been killed, Mike wouldn't have figured out the metal-concrete business. But for him, that Moonship wouldn't even be a gleam in anybody's eye. And if the Chief hadn't blown up that manned rocket we fought in the space wagons, there wouldn't be any Platform up here to reload and refuel the Moonship. So they left us behind! But just among the four of us I think we can figure that if it hadn't been for us they couldn't have made it!"

Haney grinned slowly at Joe. The Chief regarded him with irony. Mike said, "Yeah. Haney, and me, and the Chief. We did it all."

"Uh-huh," said the Chief sardonically. "Us three. Just us three. Joe didn't do anything. Just a bum, he is. We oughta tell Sally he's no good and she oughta pick herself out a guy that'll amount to something some day." He hit Joe between the shoulders. "Sure! Just a bum, Joe! That's all! But we got a weakness for you. We'll let you hang around with us just the same! Come on, guys! Let's get something to eat!"

The four of them marched down a steel-floored corridor, their magnetic-soled shoes clanking on the plates. Their progress was uncertain and ungainly and altogether undignified. Suddenly the Chief began to bawl a completely irrelevant song to the effect that the inhabitants of the kingdom of Siam were never known to wash their dishes. Haney chimed in, and Mike. They were all very close together, and they were not at all impressive. But it hit Joe very hard, this sudden knowledge that the others didn't really care. It was the first time it had occurred to him that Haney and Mike and the Chief would rather be left behind with him, as a gang, than go on to individual high achievement in a first landing on the Moon.

It felt good. It felt *real* good.

*   *   *   *   *

But that, and all other sources of satisfaction, was wiped out by news that came back from the Moonship a bare six hours later.

The Moonship was in trouble. The sequence and timing of its rocket blasts were worked out on Earth, and checked by visual and radar observation. The computations were done by electronic brains the Moonship could not possibly have carried. And everything worked out. The ship was on course and its firings were on schedule.

But then the unexpected happened. It was an error which no machine could ever have predicted, for which statistics and computations could never have compensated. It was a ***human*** error. At the signal for the final acceleration blast, the pilot of the Moonship had fired the wrong set of rockets.

Inexperience, stupidity, negligence, excitement--the reason didn't matter. After years of planning and working and dreaming, one human finger had made a mistake. And the mistake was fatal!

When the mistake was realized, they'd had sense enough to cut loose the still-firing rockets. But the damage had been done. The ship was still plunging on. It would reach the Moon. But it wouldn't land in Aristarchus crater as planned. It would crash. If every rocket remaining mounted on the hull were to be fired at the best possible instant, the Moonship would hit near Copernicus, and it would land with a terminal velocity of 800 feet per second--540 miles an hour.

It could even be calculated that when the Moonship landed, the explosion ought to be visible from Earth with a fairly good telescope. It was due to take place in thirty-two hours plus or minus a few minutes.

11

The others got the space tug into the platform's lock and did things to it, in the way of loading, that its designers never intended, while Joe was calling Earth for calculations. The result was infuriating. The Moonship had taken off for the Moon on the other side of the Platform's orbit, when it had a velocity of more than 12,000 miles an hour in the direction it wished to go. The Platform and of course the space tug was now on the reverse side of the Platform's orbit. And of course they now had a velocity of more than 12,000 miles per hour away from the direction in which it was urgently necessary for the space tug to go. They could wait for two hours to take off, said Earth, or waste the time and fuel they'd need to throw away to duplicate the effect of waiting.

"But we can't wait!" raged Joe. Then he snapped. "Look here! Suppose we take off from here, dive at Earth, make a near-graze, and let its gravity curve our course! Like a cometary path! Figure that! That's what we've got to do!"

He kicked off his magnetic-soled shoes and went diving down to the airlock. Over his shoulder he panted an order for the radar-duty man to relay anything from Earth down to him there. He arrived to find Haney and Mike in hot argument over whether it was possible to load on an extra ton or two of mass. He stopped it. They would.

"Everything's loaded?" he demanded. "Okay! Space suits! All set? Let's get out of this lock and start blasting!"

He drove them into the space tug. He climbed in himself. He closed the entrance port. The plastic walls of the lock bulged out, pulled back fast, and the steering rockets jetted. The space tug came out of the lock. It spun about. It aimed for Earth and monstrous bursts of rocket-trail spread out behind it. It dived.

Naturally! When a ship from the Platform wanted to reach Earth for atmosphere-deceleration, it was more economical to head away from it. Now that it was the most urgent of all possible necessities to get away from Earth, in the opposite direction to the space tug's present motion, it was logical to dive toward it. The ship would plunge toward Earth, and Earth's gravity would help its rockets in the attainment of frenzied speed. But the tug still possessed its orbital speed. So it would not actually strike the Earth, but would be carried eastward past its disk, even though aimed for Earth's mid-bulge. Yet Earth would continue to pull. As the space tug skimmed past, its path would be curved by the pull of gravity. At the nearest possible approach to Earth, the tug would fire its heaviest rockets for maximum acceleration. And it would swing around Earth's atmosphere perhaps no more than 500 miles high--just barely beyond the measurable presence of air--and come out of that crazy curve a good hour ahead of the Platform for a corresponding position, and with a greater velocity than could be had in any other way. Traced on paper, the course of the tug would be a tight parabola.

The ship dived. And it happened that it had left the Platform and plunged deep in Earth's shadow, so that the look and feel of things was that of an utterly suicidal plunge into oblivion. There was the seeming of a vast sack of pure blackness before the nose of the space tug. She started for it at four gravities acceleration, and Joe got his headphones to his ears and lay panting while he waited for the figures and information he had to have.

He got them. When the four-gravity rockets burned out, the tug's crew painstakingly adjusted the ship's nose to a certain position. They flung themselves back into the acceleration chairs and Joe fired a six-g blast. They came out of that, and he fired another. The three blasts gave the ship a downward speed of a mile and a half a second, and Earth's pull added to it steadily. The Earth itself was drawing them down most of a 4,000-mile fall, which added to the speed their rockets built up.

Down on Earth, radar-bowls wavered dizzily, hunting for them to feed them observations of position and data for their guidance. Back on the Platform, members of the crew feverishly made their own computations. When the four in the Space tug were half-way to Earth, they were traveling faster than any humans had ever traveled before, relative to the Earth or the Platform itself. When they were a thousand miles from Earth, it was certain they would clear its edge. Joe proposed and received an okay to fire a salvo of Mark Tens to speed the ship still more. When they burned to the release-point and flashed away past the ports, the Chief and Haney panted up from their chairs and made their way aft.

"Going to reload the firing-frames," gasped the Chief.

They vanished. The space tug could take rockets from its cargo and set them outside its hull for firing. No other ship could.

Haney and the Chief came back. There was dead silence in the ship, save for a small, tinny voice in Joe's headphones.

"We'll pass Earth 600 miles high," said Joe in a flat voice. "Maybe closer. I'm going to try to make it 450. We'll be smack over enemy territory, but I doubt they could hit us. We'll be hitting better than six miles a second. If we wanted to, we could spend some more rockets and hit escape velocity. But we want to stop, later. We'll ride it out."

Silence. Stillness. Speed. Out the ports to Earthward there was purest blackness. On the other side, a universe of stars. But the blackness grew and grew and grew until it neatly bisected the cosmos itself, and half of everything that was, was blackness. Half was tiny colored stars.

Then there was a sound. A faint sound. It was a moan. It was a howl. It was a shriek.... And then it was a mere thin moan again. Then it was not.

"We touched air," said Joe calmly, "at six and a quarter miles per second. Pretty thin, though. At that, we may have left a meteor-trail for the populace to admire."

Nobody said anything at all. In a little while there was light ahead. There was brightness. Instantly, it seemed, they were out of night and there was a streaming tumult of clouds flashing past below--but they were 800 miles up now--and Joe's headphones rattled and he said:

"Now we can give a touch of course-correction, and maybe a trace of speed...."

Rockets droned and boomed and roared outside the hull. The Earth fell away and away and presently it was behind. And they were plunging on after the Moon-ship which was very, very, very far on before them.

It was actually many hours before they reached it. They couldn't afford to over-take it gradually, because they had to have time to work in after contact. But over-taking it swiftly cost extra fuel, and they hadn't too much. So they compromised, and came up behind the Moonship at better than 2,000 feet per second difference in speed--they approached it as fast as most rifle-bullets travel--and all creation was blotted out by the fumes of the rockets they fired for deceleration.

Then the space tug came cautiously close to the Moonship. Mike climbed out on the outside of the tug's hull, with the Chief also in space equipment, paying out Mike's safety-line. Mike leaped across two hundred yards of emptiness with light-years of gulf beneath him. His metal soles clanked on the Moonship's hull.

Then the vision-screen on the tug lighted up. Lieutenant Commander Brown looked out of it, quietly grim. Joe flicked on his own transmitter. He nodded.

"*Mr. Kenmore*," said Brown evenly, "*I did not contact you before because I was not certain that contact could be made. How many passengers can you take back to the Platform?*"

Joe blinked at him.

"I haven't any idea," he said. "But I'm going to hitch on and use our rockets to land you."

"*I do not think it practicable*," said Brown calmly. "*I believe the only result of such a course will be the loss of both ships with all hands. I will give you a written authorization to return on my order. But since all my crew can't return, how many can you take? I have ten married men aboard. Six have children. Can you take six? Or all ten?"* Then he said without a trace of emphasis, *"Of course, none of them will be officers."*

"If I tried to turn back now, I think my crew would mutiny," Joe said coldly. "I'd hate to think they wouldn't, anyhow! We're going to hook on and play this out the way it lies!"

There was a pause. Then Brown spoke again. *"Mr. Kenmore, I was hoping you'd say that. Actually--er--not to be quoted, you understand--actually, intelligent defiance has always been in the traditions of the Navy. Of course, you're not in the Navy, Kenmore, but right now it looks like the Navy is in your hands. Like a battleship in the hands of a tug. Good luck, Kenmore."*

Joe flicked off the screen. "You know," he said, winking at Mike, "I guess Brown isn't such a bad egg after all. Let's go!"

In minutes, the space tug had a line made fast. In half an hour, the two space craft were bound firmly together, but far enough apart for the rocket blasts to dissipate before they reached the Moonship. Mike returned to the tug. A pair of the big Mark Twenty rockets burned frenziedly in emptiness.

The Moonship was slowed by a fraction of its speed. The deceleration was hardly perceptible.

There were more burnings. Back on Earth there were careful measurements. A tight beam tends to attenuate when it is thrown a hundred thousand miles. It tends to! When speech is conducted over it, the lag between comment and reply is perceptible. It's not great--just over half a second. But one notices it. That lag was used to measure the speed and distance of the two craft. The prospect didn't look too good.

The space tug burned rocket after rocket after rocket. There was no effect that Joe could detect, of course. It would have been like noticing the effect of single oar-strokes in a rowboat miles from shore. But the instruments on Earth found a difference. They made very, very, very careful computations. And the electronic brains did the calculations which battalions of mathematicians would have needed years to work out. The electronic calculations which could not make a mistake said--that it was a toss-up.

The Moon came slowly to float before the two linked ships. It grew slowly, slowly larger. The word from Earth was that considering the rockets still available in the space tug, and those that should have been fired but weren't on the Moonship, there must be no more blasts just yet. The two ships must pass together through the neutral-point where the gravities of Earth and Moon exactly cancel out. They must fall together toward the Moon. Forty miles above the lunar surface such-and-such rockets were to be fired. At twenty miles, such-and-such others. At five miles the Moonship itself must fire its remaining fuel-store. With luck, it was a toss-up. Safety or a smash.

But there was a long time to wait. Joe and his crew relaxed in the space tug. The Chief looked out a port and observed:

"I can see the ring-mountains now. Naked-eye stuff, too! I wonder if anybody ever saw that before!"

"Not likely," said Joe.

Mike stared out a port. Haney looked, also.

"How're we going to get back, Joe?"

"The Moonship has rockets on board," Joe told him. "Only they can't stick them in the firing-racks outside. They're stowed away, all shipshape, Navy fashion. After we land, we'll ask politely for rockets to get back to the Platform with. It'll be a tedious run. Mostly coasting--falling free. But we'll make it."

"If everything doesn't blow when we land," said the Chief.

Joe said uncomfortably: "It won't. Not that somebody won't try." Then he stopped. After a moment he said awkwardly: "Look! It's necessary that we humans get to the stars, or ultimately we'll crowd the Earth until we won't be able to stay human. We'd have to have wars and plagues and such things to keep our numbers down. It--it seems to me, and I--think it's been said before, that it looks like there's something, somewhere, that's afraid of us humans. It doesn't want us to reach the stars. It didn't want us to fly. Before that it didn't want us to learn how to cure disease, or have steam, or--anything that makes men different from the beasts."

Haney turned his head. He listened intently.

"Maybe it sounds--superstitious," said Joe uneasily, "but there's always been somebody trying to smash everything the rest of us wanted. As if--as if something alien and hateful went around whispering hypnotically into men's ears while they slept, commanding them irresistibly to do things to smash all their own hopes."

The Chief grunted. "Huh! D'you think that's new stuff, Joe?"

"N-no," admitted Joe. "But it's true. Something fights us. You can make wild guesses. Maybe--things on far planets that know that if ever we reach there.... There's something that hates men and it tries to make us destroy ourselves."

"Sure," said Haney mildly. "I learned about that in Sunday School, Joe."

"Maybe I mean that," said Joe helplessly. "But anyhow there's something we fight--and there's Something that fights with us. So I think we're going to get the Moonship down all right."

Mike said sharply: "You mean you think this is all worked out in advance. That we'd be here, we'd get here----"

The Chief said impatiently, "It's figured out so we can do it if we got the innards. We got the chance. We can duck it. But if we duck it, it's bad, and somebody else has to have the chance later. I know what Joe's saying. Us men, we got to get to the stars. There's millions of 'em, and we need the planets they've got swimming around 'em."

Haney said, "Some of them have planets. That's known. Yeah."

"Those planets ain't going to go on forever with nobody using 'em," grunted the Chief. "It don't make sense. And things in general do make sense. All but us humans," he finished with a grin. "And I like us, anyhow. Joe's right. We'll get by this time. And if we don't--some other guys'll have to do the job of landing on the Moon. But it'll be done--as a starter."

"I can see lots of mountains down there. Plain," Mike said quietly.

"What's the radar say?"

Joe looked. Back at the Platform it had shown the curve of the surface of Earth. Here a dim line was beginning to show on the vertical-plane screen. It was the curve of the surface of the Moon.

"We might as well get set," said Joe. "We've got time but we might as well. Space suits on. I'll tighten up the chain. Steering rockets'll do that. Then we'll take a last look. All firing racks loaded outside?"

"Yeah," said Haney. He grinned wrily. "You know, Joe, I know what I know, but still I'm scared."

"Me, too," said Joe.

But there were things to do. They took their places. They watched out the ports. The Moon had seemed a vast round ball a little while back. Now it appeared to be flattening. Its edges still curved away beyond a surprisingly nearby horizon. The ring-mountains were amazingly distinct. There were incredibly wide, smooth spaces with mottled colorings. But the mountains....

When the ships were 40 miles high the space tug blasted valorously, and all the panorama of the Moon's surface was momentarily hidden by the racing clouds of mist. The rockets burned out.

Haney and the Chief replaced the burned-out rockets. They were gigantic, heavy-bore tubes which they couldn't have stirred on Earth. Now they loaded them into the curious locks which conveyed them outside the hull into firing position.

The ring-mountains were gigantic when they blasted again! They were only 20 miles up, then, and some of the peaks rose four miles from their inner crater floors.

The ships were still descending fast. Joe spoke into his microphone.

"Calling Moonship! Calling----" He stopped and said matter-of-factly, "I suggest we fire our last blast together. Shall I give the word? Right!"

The surface of the Moon came toward them. Craters, cracks, frozen fountains of stone, swelling undulations of ground interrupted without rhyme or reason by the gigantic splashings of missiles from the sky a hundred thousand million years ago. The colorings were unbelievable. There were reds and browns and yellows. There were grays and dusty deep-blues and streaks of completely impossible tints in combination.

But Joe couldn't watch that. He kept his eyes on a very special gadget which was a radar range-finder. He hadn't used it about the Platform because there were too many tin cans and such trivia floating about. It wouldn't be dependable. But it did measure the exact distance to the nearest solid object.

"Prepare for firing on a count of five," said Joe quietly. "Five ... four ... three ... two ... one ... fire!"

The space tug's rockets blasted. For the first time since they overtook the Moonship, the tug now had help. The remaining rockets outside the Moonship's hull blasted furiously. Out the ports there was nothing but hurtling whitenesses. The rockets droned and rumbled and roared....

The main rockets burned out. The steering rockets still boomed. Joe had thrown them on for what good their lift might do.

"Joe!" said Haney in a surprised tone. "I feel weight! Not much, but some! And the main rockets are off!"

Joe nodded. He watched the instruments before him. He shifted a control, and the space tug swayed. It swayed over to the limit of the tow-chain it had fastened to the Moonship. Joe shifted his controls again.

There was a peculiar, gritty contact somewhere. Joe cut the steering rockets and it was possible to look out. There were more gritty noises. The space tug settled a little and leaned a little. It was still. Then there was no noise at all.

"Yes," said Joe. "We've got some weight. We're on the Moon."

They went out of the ship in a peculiarly solemn procession. About them reared cliffs such as no man had ever looked on before save in dreams. Above their heads hung a huge round greenish globe, with a white polar ice-cap plainly visible. It hung in mid-sky and was four times the size of the Moon as seen from Earth. If one stood still and looked at it, it would undoubtedly be seen to be revolving, once in some twenty-four hours.

Mike scuffled in the dust in which he walked. Nobody had emerged from the Moonship yet. The four of them were literally the first human beings ever to set foot on the surface of the Moon. But none of them mentioned the fact, though all were acutely aware of it. Mike kicked up dust. It rose in a curiously liquid-like fashion. There was no air to scatter it. It settled deliberately back again.

Mike spoke with an odd constraint. "No green cheese," he said absurdly.

"No," agreed Joe. "Let's go over to the Moonship. It looks all right. It couldn't have landed hard."

They went toward the bulk of the ship from Earth, which now was a base for the military occupation of a globe with more land-area than all Earth's continents put together--but not a drop of water. The Moonship was tilted slightly askew, but it was patently unharmed. There were faces at every port in the hull.

The Chief stopped suddenly. A sizable boulder rose from the dust. The Chief struck it smartly with his space-gloved hand.

"I'm counting coup on the Moon!" he said zestfully "Tie that, you guys!"

Then he joined the others on their way to the Moonship's main lock.

"Shall we knock?" asked Mike humorously. "I doubt they've got a door-bell!" But the lock-door was opening to admit them. They crowded inside.

Commander Brown was waiting for them with an out-stretched hand. "Glad to have you aboard." And there was a genuine smile creeping across his face.

*   *   *   *   *

Joe talked with careful distinctness into a microphone. His voice took a little over a second to reach its destination. Then there was a pause of the same length before the first syllable of Sally's reply came to him from Earth.

"I've reported to your father," said Joe carefully, "and the Moonship has reported to the Navy. In a couple of hours Haney and the Chief and Mike and I will be taking off to go back to the Platform. We got rockets from the stores of the Moonship."

Sally's voice was surprisingly clear. It wavered a little, but there was no sound of static to mar reception.

"Then what, Joe?"

"I'm bringing written reports and photographs and first specimens of geology from the Moon," Joe told her. "I'm a mailman. It'll probably be sixty hours back to the Platform--free fall most of the way--and then we'll refuel and I'll come down to Earth to deliver the reports and such."

Pause. One second and a little for his voice to go. Another second and something over for her voice to return.

"And then?"

"That's what I'm trying to find out," said Joe. "What day is today?"

"Tuesday," said Sally after the inevitable pause. "It's ten o'clock Tuesday morning at the Shed."

Joe made calculations in his mind. Then he said:

"I ought to land on Earth some time next Monday."

Pause.

"Yes?" said Sally.

"I wondered," said Joe. "How about a date that night?" Another pause. Then Sally's voice. She sounded glad.

"It's a date, Joe. And--do you know, I must be the first girl in the world to make a date with the Man in the Moon?"

COMBAT MISSION!

Joe Kenmore's mission was as dangerous as it sounded simple:

"DELIVER SUPPLIES AND ATOMIC WEAPONS TO THE SPACE
 PLATFORM.
THEN PREPARE FOR MAN'S FIRST EXPEDITION TO THE MOON."

Joe had helped launch the first Space Platform--that initial rung in man's ladder to the stars. But the enemies who had ruthlessly tried to destroy the space station before it left Earth were still at work. They were plotting to stop Joe's mission!

Cover painting by Robert Schulz

The Codes Of Hammurabi And Moses
W. W. Davies

QTY

The discovery of the Hammurabi Code is one of the greatest achievements of archaeology, and is of paramount interest, not only to the student of the Bible, but also to all those interested in ancient history...

Religion   **ISBN:** *1-59462-338-4*   **Pages:132**

MSRP $12.95

The Theory of Moral Sentiments
Adam Smith

QTY

This work from 1749. contains original theories of conscience amd moral judgment and it is the foundation for systemof morals.

Philosophy   **ISBN:** *1-59462-777-0*   **Pages:536**

MSRP $19.95

Jessica's First Prayer
Hesba Stretton

QTY

In a screened and secluded corner of one of the many railway-bridges which span the streets of London there could be seen a few years ago, from five o'clock every morning until half past eight, a tidily set-out coffee-stall, consisting of a trestle and board, upon which stood two large tin cans, with a small fire of charcoal burning under each so as to keep the coffee boiling during the early hours of the morning when the work-people were thronging into the city on their way to their daily toil...

Childrens   **ISBN:** *1-59462-373-2*   **Pages:84**

MSRP $9.95

My Life and Work
Henry Ford

QTY

Henry Ford revolutionized the world with his implementation of mass production for the Model T automobile. Gain valuable business insight into his life and work with his own auto-biography... "We have only started on our development of our country we have not as yet, with all our talk of wonderful progress, done more than scratch the surface. The progress has been wonderful enough but..."

Biographies/   **ISBN:** *1-59462-198-5*   **Pages:300**

MSRP $21.95

The Art of Cross-Examination
Francis Wellman

QTY

I presume it is the experience of every author, after his first book is published upon an important subject, to be almost overwhelmed with a wealth of ideas and illustrations which could readily have been included in his book, and which to his own mind, at least, seem to make a second edition inevitable. Such certainly was the case with me; and when the first edition had reached its sixth impression in five months, I rejoiced to learn that it seemed to my publishers that the book had met with a sufficiently favorable reception to justify a second and considerably enlarged edition. ..

Pages:412

Reference   **ISBN:** *1-59462-647-2*   *MSRP $19.95*

On the Duty of Civil Disobedience
Henry David Thoreau

QTY

Thoreau wrote his famous essay, On the Duty of Civil Disobedience, as a protest against an unjust but popular war and the immoral but popular institution of slave-owning. He did more than write—he declined to pay his taxes, and was hauled off to gaol in consequence. Who can say how much this refusal of his hastened the end of the war and of slavery ?

Law   **ISBN:** *1-59462-747-9*   **Pages:48**

MSRP $7.45

Dream Psychology Psychoanalysis for Beginners
Sigmund Freud

QTY

Sigmund Freud, born Sigismund Schlomo Freud (May 6, 1856 - September 23, 1939), was a Jewish-Austrian neurologist and psychiatrist who co-founded the psychoanalytic school of psychology. Freud is best known for his theories of the unconscious mind, especially involving the mechanism of repression; his redefinition of sexual desire as mobile and directed towards a wide variety of objects; and his therapeutic techniques, especially his understanding of transference in the therapeutic relationship and the presumed value of dreams as sources of insight into unconscious desires.

Pages:196

Psychology   **ISBN:** *1-59462-905-6*   *MSRP $15.45*

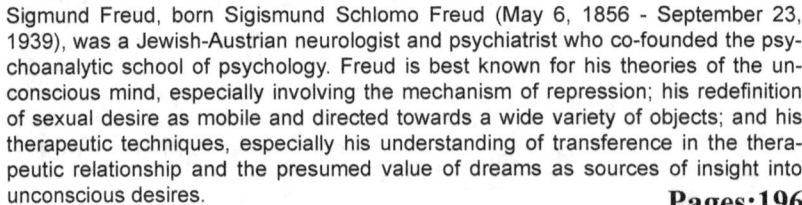

The Miracle of Right Thought
Orison Swett Marden

QTY

Believe with all of your heart that you will do what you were made to do. When the mind has once formed the habit of holding cheerful, happy, prosperous pictures, it will not be easy to form the opposite habit. It does not matter how improbable or how far away this realization may see, or how dark the prospects may be, if we visualize them as best we can, as vividly as possible, hold tenaciously to them and vigorously struggle to attain them, they will gradually become actualized, realized in the life. But a desire, a longing without endeavor, a yearning abandoned or held indifferently will vanish without realization.

Pages:360

Self Help   **ISBN:** *1-59462-644-8*   *MSRP $25.45*

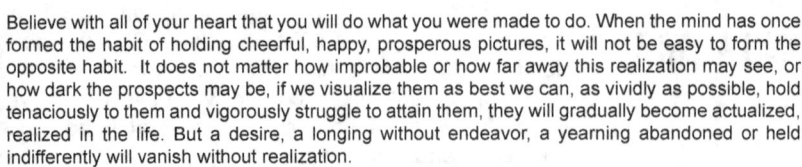

QTY

The Rosicrucian Cosmo-Conception Mystic Christianity by *Max Heindel*   ISBN: *1-59462-188-8* **$38.95**
The Rosicrucian Cosmo-conception is not dogmatic, neither does it appeal to any other authority than the reason of the student. It is: not controversial, but is: sent forth in the, hope that it may help to clear...   New Age/Religion Pages 646

Abandonment To Divine Providence by *Jean-Pierre de Caussade*   ISBN: *1-59462-228-0* **$25.95**
"The Rev. Jean Pierre de Caussade was one of the most remarkable spiritual writers of the Society of Jesus in France in the 18th Century. His death took place at Toulouse in 1751. His works have gone through many editions and have been republished...   Inspirational/Religion Pages 400

Mental Chemistry by *Charles Haanel*   ISBN: *1-59462-192-6* **$23.95**
Mental Chemistry allows the change of material conditions by combining and appropriately utilizing the power of the mind. Much like applied chemistry creates something new and unique out of careful combinations of chemicals the mastery of mental chemistry...   New Age Pages 354

The Letters of Robert Browning and Elizabeth Barret Barrett 1845-1846 vol II   ISBN: *1-59462-193-4* **$35.95**
by *Robert Browning* and *Elizabeth Barrett*   Biographies Pages 596

Gleanings In Genesis (volume I) by *Arthur W. Pink*   ISBN: *1-59462-130-6* **$27.45**
Appropriately has Genesis been termed "the seed plot of the Bible" for in it we have, in germ form, almost all of the great doctrines which are afterwards fully developed in the books of Scripture which follow...   Religion/Inspirational Pages 420

The Master Key by *L. W. de Laurence*   ISBN: *1-59462-001-6* **$30.95**
In no branch of human knowledge has there been a more lively increase of the spirit of research during the past few years than in the study of Psychology, Concentration and Mental Discipline. The requests for authentic lessons in Thought Control, Mental Discipline and...   New Age/Business Pages 422

The Lesser Key Of Solomon Goetia by *L. W. de Laurence*   ISBN: *1-59462-092-X* **$9.95**
This translation of the first book of the "Lernegton" which is now for the first time made accessible to students of Talismanic Magic was done, after careful collation and edition, from numerous Ancient Manuscripts in Hebrew, Latin, and French...   New Age/Occult Pages 92

Rubaiyat Of Omar Khayyam by *Edward Fitzgerald*   ISBN:*1-59462-332-5* **$13.95**
Edward Fitzgerald, whom the world has already learned, in spite of his own efforts to remain within the shadow of anonymity, to look upon as one of the rarest poets of the century, was born at Bredfield, in Suffolk, on the 31st of March, 1809. He was the third son of John Purcell...   Music Pages 172

Ancient Law by *Henry Maine*   ISBN: *1-59462-128-4* **$29.95**
The chief object of the following pages is to indicate some of the earliest ideas of mankind, as they are reflected in Ancient Law, and to point out the relation of those ideas to modern thought.   Religion/History Pages 452

Far-Away Stories by *William J. Locke*   ISBN: *1-59462-129-2* **$19.45**
"Good wine needs no bush, but a collection of mixed vintages does. And this book is just such a collection. Some of the stories I do not want to remain buried for ever in the museum files of dead magazine-numbers an author's not unpardonable vanity..."   Fiction Pages 272

Life of David Crockett by *David Crockett*   ISBN: *1-59462-250-7* **$27.45**
"Colonel David Crockett was one of the most remarkable men of the times in which he lived. Born in humble life, but gifted with a strong will, an indomitable courage, and unremitting perseverance...   Biographies/New Age Pages 424

Lip-Reading by *Edward Nitchie*   ISBN: *1-59462-206-X* **$25.95**
Edward B. Nitchie, founder of the New York School for the Hard of Hearing, now the Nitchie School of Lip-Reading, Inc, wrote "LIP-READING Principles and Practice". The development and perfecting of this meritorious work on lip-reading was an undertaking...   How-to Pages 400

A Handbook of Suggestive Therapeutics, Applied Hypnotism, Psychic Science   ISBN: *1-59462-214-0* **$24.95**
by *Henry Munro*   Health/New Age/Health/Self-help Pages 376

A Doll's House: and Two Other Plays by *Henrik Ibsen*   ISBN: *1-59462-112-8* **$19.95**
Henrik Ibsen created this classic when in revolutionary 1848 Rome. Introducing some striking concepts in playwriting for the realist genre, this play has been studied the world over.   Fiction/Classics/Plays 308

The Light of Asia by *sir Edwin Arnold*   ISBN: *1-59462-204-3* **$13.95**
In this poetic masterpiece, Edwin Arnold describes the life and teachings of Buddha. The man who was to become known as Buddha to the world was born as Prince Gautama of India but he rejected the worldly riches and abandoned the reigns of power when...   Religion/History/Biographies Pages 170

The Complete Works of Guy de Maupassant by *Guy de Maupassant*   ISBN: *1-59462-157-8* **$16.95**
"For days and days, nights and nights, I had dreamed of that first kiss which was to consecrate our engagement, and I knew not on what spot I should put my lips..."   Fiction/Classics Pages 240

The Art of Cross-Examination by *Francis L. Wellman*   ISBN: *1-59462-309-0* **$26.95**
Written by a renowned trial lawyer, Wellman imparts his experience and uses case studies to explain how to use psychology to extract desired information through questioning.   How-to/Science/Reference Pages 408

Answered or Unanswered? by *Louisa Vaughan*   ISBN: *1-59462-248-5* **$10.95**
Miracles of Faith in China   Religion Pages 112

The Edinburgh Lectures on Mental Science (1909) by *Thomas*   ISBN: *1-59462-008-3* **$11.95**
This book contains the substance of a course of lectures recently given by the writer in the Queen Street Hall, Edinburgh. Its purpose is to indicate the Natural Principles governing the relation between Mental Action and Material Conditions...   New Age/Psychology Pages 148

Ayesha by *H. Rider Haggard*   ISBN: *1-59462-301-5* **$24.95**
Verily and indeed it is the unexpected that happens! Probably if there was one person upon the earth from whom the Editor of this, and of a certain previous history, did not expect to hear again...   Classics Pages 380

Ayala's Angel by *Anthony Trollope*   ISBN: *1-59462-352-X* **$29.95**
The two girls were both pretty, but Lucy who was twenty-one who supposed to be simple and comparatively unattractive, whereas Ayala was credited, as her Bombwhat romantic name might show, with poetic charm and a taste for romance. Ayala when her father died was nineteen...   Fiction Pages 484

The American Commonwealth by *James Bryce*   ISBN: *1-59462-286-8* **$34.45**
An interpretation of American democratic political theory. It examines political mechanics and society from the perspective of Scotsman James Bryce   Politics Pages 572

Stories of the Pilgrims by *Margaret P. Pumphrey*   ISBN: *1-59462-116-0* **$17.95**
This book explores pilgrims religious oppression in England as well as their escape to Holland and eventual crossing to America on the Mayflower, and their early days in New England...   History Pages 268

QTY

The Fasting Cure *by Sinclair Upton*   ISBN: *1-59462-222-1* **$13.95**
In the Cosmopolitan Magazine for May, 1910, and in the Contemporary Review (London) for April, 1910 I published an article dealing with my experiences in fasting. I have written a great many magazine articles, but never one which attracted so much attention... New Age/Self Help/Health Pages 164

Hebrew Astrology *by Sepharial*   ISBN: *1-59462-308-2* **$13.45**
In these days of advanced thinking it is a matter of common observation that we have left many of the old landmarks behind and that we are now pressing forward to greater heights and to a wider horizon than that which represented the mind-content of our progenitors... Astrology Pages 144

Thought Vibration or The Law of Attraction in the Thought World   ISBN: *1-59462-127-6* **$12.95**
by William Walker Atkinson   Psychology/Religion Pages 144

Optimism *by Helen Keller*   ISBN: *1-59462-108-X* **$15.95**
Helen Keller was blind, deaf, and mute since 19 months old, yet famously learned how to overcome these handicaps, communicate with the world, and spread her lectures promoting optimism. An inspiring read for everyone... Biographies/Inspirational Pages 84

Sara Crewe *by Frances Burnett*   ISBN: *1-59462-360-0* **$9.45**
In the first place, Miss Minchin lived in London. Her home was a large, dull, tall one, in a large, dull square, where all the houses were alike, and all the sparrows were alike, and where all the door-knockers made the same heavy sound... Childrens/Classic Pages 88

The Autobiography of Benjamin Franklin *by Benjamin Franklin*   ISBN: *1-59462-135-7* **$24.95**
The Autobiography of Benjamin Franklin has probably been more extensively read than any other American historical work, and no other book of its kind has had such ups and downs of fortune. Franklin lived for many years in England, where he was agent... Biographies/History Pages 332

Name	
Email	
Telephone	
Address	
City, State ZIP	

☐ **Credit Card**   ☐ **Check / Money Order**

Credit Card Number	
Expiration Date	
Signature	

Please Mail to: Book Jungle
                     PO Box 2226
                     Champaign, IL 61825
or Fax to: 630-214-0564

ORDERING INFORMATION

web: *www.bookjungle.com*
email: *sales@bookjungle.com*
fax: *630-214-0564*
mail: *Book Jungle PO Box 2226 Champaign, IL 61825*
or PayPal *to sales@bookjungle.com*

Please contact us for bulk discounts

DIRECT-ORDER TERMS

**20% Discount if You Order
Two or More Books**
Free Domestic Shipping!
Accepted: Master Card, Visa,
Discover, American Express